His Name Was Arthur

By

Leah Toole

His Name Was Arthur

Also by Leah Toole

The Tudor Heirs Series

I – The Saddest Princess

...

II – The Haunted Queen

...

III – The Puppet King

...

IV – The Forgotten Prince

...

V – The Hopeful Duke

~

The Rose and the Pomegranate

~

1500

~

All That Life

Foreword

What constitutes a meaningful life?
Is it one's achievements, accomplished through years of hardship and struggle; or perhaps it's one's sacrifices, made for loved ones, or for the greater good.
But what of the lives that were unable to reach their potential? Those who were cut short due to unexpected circumstances.
Are they less meaningful because they did not achieve their purpose? Or is one's journey – however short – what constitutes life's meaning?
Their traces left behind bearing the blueprints of the future…

Prologue

<u>20th September 1486</u>

They named him Arthur.

Arthur – after the great hero of British mythology, King Arthur of Camelot, a name which held great significance and instilled high hopes for the future and the Tudor dynasty as a whole.

It was the perfect choice for a prince that promised a new era of stability with but his mere existence.

His name was chosen before he was even born, before his mother and father even knew that he would be a boy, so great was the desire for their firstborn to be male. And soon, all of England would learn of it.

<u>24th September 1486</u>
<u>Winchester Cathedral</u>

On a cold and wet day, England's nobility and its people assembled in Winchester Cathedral to celebrate the birth of the new king and queen's first child.

An outpouring of joy and festivity was felt throughout the entire country following this child's birth four days prior, not only for the announcement that it was healthy and strong, but also because it was a boy.

"God smiles down on the new king!"

"In only thirteen months on the throne, King Henry has married favourably and already obtained an heir!"

The people's excited chatter was heard throughout the city of London, aristocrats and common folk alike basking in their sovereign's glory.

But no one was as delighted as the king and queen themselves, for with their prince's birth they had achieved the first step in securing the Tudor succession and solidifying the peace that Henry Tudor had promised to bring to England.

The cathedral was decorated with expensive arras tapestries depicting biblical stories, woven richly with gold and silk thread. An elevated stage had been built to support the silver font where the child would be christened, a nearby brazier fire glowing brightly to keep the day's chill at bay.

Guarding the access to the dais were senior yeomen of the crown, standing modishly in their grand attire, a mixture of both Yorkists and Lancastrians to demonstrate to the public that the former Houses who had once opposed each other during the bloody years of the Cousins' War would co-exist harmoniously under Henry Tudor's reign.

The procession began, being led by one hundred henchmen of the king's hall, esquires, and gentlemen of the crown, all carrying unlit torches in rows of two-by-two. Following them came twenty-six chaplains and clerics of the Chapel Royal, who chanted harmoniously as they walked slowly towards the font, their voices echoing throughout the cathedral.

The honour of carrying the prince went to his aunt, Princess Cecily, who held him tightly against her chest as though he were the most precious thing in all the realm.

Which, of course, he was.

The prince, just four days old, blinked up at his aunt's face as she smiled at him. He yawned drowsily, then scrunched up his eyes, his skin turning red with frustration. But his aunt bounced him expertly in her arms, the warmth of her embrace and the gentle lull of the church's song soothing him back to sleep.

He was wrapped in a beautiful mantle of crimson cloth of gold furred with ermine – which Princess Cecily tucked up to his little chin as his eyes fluttered closed – and a train so long it needed supporting by four nobles as he made his way towards the font.

The one hundred torches were lit then, as the boy was brought to the font, and the Bishop of Worcester John Alcock performed the christening. Baby Arthur slept peacefully throughout.

And the hundreds of delighted onlookers watched from their pews in silent awe, the sweet scent of frankincense hanging in the air, and the golden glow of hope for the future rekindled in their hearts.

Part 1

Legacy

Chapter 1

<u>One year earlier</u>

<u>22ⁿᵈ August 1485</u>
<u>Bosworth Field, Leicestershire</u>

King Richard III was dead.

His broken body was stripped bare and flung over the back of a horse, his arms and legs hanging down its sides.

There was no dignity shown to the last Plantagenet King.

His victor, the Welshman Henry Tudor, knelt down on one knee in the middle of the battlefield, mud-splattered and breathless, to receive the king's circlet which had been retrieved from among the chaos. Clad in full-body armour, Henry Tudor bowed his dark head to receive the honour he had fought so valiantly for.

"Judge me, oh Lord, and favour my cause," he mumbled as he stared down at the ground, blood and dirt mixing into an ominous maroon hue. The enormity of this moment clutched at his heart. His reign had begun in violence, and it was up to him to make sure it would not seep into his sovereignty.

Henry Tudor had gained the crown through right of conquest, and his victory marked the end of the thirty-year-long Cousin's War. Or, at least, the first step towards achieving that promise.

A cheer broke out from his men, thousands of roars echoing in the wind, hailing their new Lancastrian King.

He stood and looked about himself, holding his head high and drinking in the men's cheers. A quirk tugged at the side of his mouth, pride blooming inside of him at what he had accomplished that day.

And yet, though the battle that gained him the crown had been a glorious success, Henry Tudor's real struggle was about to begin. Because kingship was never as golden as it was believed to be.

<u>Sheriff Hutton Castle, Yorkshire</u>

Elizabeth of York, eldest daughter to the late King Edward IV, stood staring out of the window, too nervous to entertain even the prospect of distraction. Sunlight had slipped away from yet another day, leaving the world in a purple darkness, extinguishing any hope she'd had for word of what was to become of her and her family.

"He will come," a voice said, and she turned towards the sound.

"Mother," she said, acknowledging her presence.

Elizabeth Woodville, the widowed queen of Edward IV, approached her daughter by the window.

"He has based his claim to the throne," she said, hoping to soothe her nervous eldest child, "on the promise that he marries you and unites the Houses of York and Lancaster. On the promise that he will end the wars."

She knew it to be true, but unease stirred within the young woman's belly nonetheless, a vexed snake coiling around itself, hissing doubt into her veins.

She did not think she could face another day of waiting. It was all she had done for two days following the news that her uncle, King Richard III, had been defeated in battle. But waiting was all she *could* do, for she was not the decider of her fate. No woman ever truly was.

"Have you heard from the Lady Margaret Beaufort?" the young woman asked, her gentle voice hitching with the nervousness she could not tamper.

Elizabeth Woodville shook her head, "No. But fret not, Lizzie. Your betrothal to Henry Tudor has been promised long ago.

Margaret Beaufort, his mother, will not go back on her word. This match benefits us all."

"You know as well as I that kings go back on their word," Lizzie countered as she turned away and watched as a bat flittered sporadically past the window, blind and uncertain of its path. She could sympathise with its panic, could practically *feel* its disorientation.

Lizzie did not need to elaborate, for her mother knew of what she spoke. The former king, Richard III, had also made promises. Namely, to keep his nephews – Lizzie's brothers, and Edward IV's sons – safe when he placed them in the Tower of London. Instead, Parliament had passed an Act that declared Edward IV's marriage to Elizabeth Woodville as invalid, thereby proclaiming all their children as illegitimate, and the throne had fallen to Edward IV's brother Richard by default.

Richard had done nothing to stop it, of course. For why would he? Parliament's decision had that day made him King of England. And Richard was nothing if not a stickler for the rules. But shortly thereafter, the two young princes that had been put in Richard's care had mysteriously vanished from the Tower of London. And rumours of *who* had made them disappear did not take long to form.

"He will come," her mother repeated presently, as though trying to convince herself. Or in an effort to ignore Lizzie's remark, for the wound of her sons' disappearances was still too fresh.

"Give him time," the former queen continued, "There is much that needs to be done before he presents himself to you. Tudor is likely rectifying your uncle Richard's wrongdoings as we speak, and restoring your legitimacy so that you may be wed."

Lizzie turned to face her namesake, the mirror image of herself; though age and grief had not yet taken its toll on her exterior the way it had her mother's.

"But even then," Lizzie said, "what if this union does not end it? The country's unrest."

Her mother inhaled deeply as she thought, "Henry Tudor is a Lancastrian. You are a Yorkist. By uniting before God, nobody will have any cause for uproar. No one will have a greater claim to the English throne than the two of you, together."

Lizzie hesitated, noticing that her mother had avoided her question.

She turned to stare out the window again, listening intently for any sign of his approach. But she heard only the rustle of wind in the trees and a dog barking yonder. And the snake in her belly writhed tighter, spitting venom.

"Your marriage to Tudor will be enough to settle those who would oppose him as the new king," Elizabeth Woodville assured, taking her twenty-year-old daughter's hand and squeezing it.

Lizzie looked down at their intertwined fingers, hoping to draw strength from her mother's higher wisdom. And then, just as she was about to resign herself to another sleepless night, her blue eyes caught movement in the twilight, followed by the unmistakeable thunder of horse hooves growing louder with the king's arrival.

"My Lady," the new king said a short while later as he bowed his head at the young woman who was to be his bride.

Lizzie curtsied elegantly in response, briefly meeting his gaze before looking shyly at the stone floor between them.

"Your Grace."

He was tall, Lizzie noted as she straightened up, with shoulder-length, auburn hair and angular features. He was not quite as intimidating as she had feared, not half as unsightly as she'd envisioned.

The king cleared his throat, then looked over his shoulder at his entourage, and with a slight nod, urged one forward.

Lizzie recognised some of the men, in particular William and Thomas Stanley, both former courtiers of her father, Edward IV, and even of her uncle, Richard III.

From what she understood, they had been loyal to the Yorks but had quickly swapped sides at Bosworth Field when her uncle's grip on the crown had begun to fail. Lizzie heard that it was William Stanley's last-minute decision to support Tudor which had aided in winning him the battle, Stanley's troops tipping the scale in Tudor's favour.

But neither of the Stanley brothers stepped forward, and instead, a man Lizzie did not recognise addressed her and her mother.

He was older, with a cropped, grey beard. But underneath the beard, Lizzie saw the hint of a smile, and her shoulders relaxed a little.

"His Highness has arranged for you, your mother and sisters to be moved to Coldharbour," he said with a bow of his head, his voice deep and oddly reassuring, "for your comfort and protection."

"I hear Coldharbour is now the property of the Lady Margaret Beaufort," Elizabeth Woodville answered from beside Lizzie.

The bearded man bent at the waist at the Dowager Queen's words, "Your Grace," he murmured in acknowledgement, and Lizzie was pleased to hear respect in his voice.

"Jasper Tudor," her mother replied in greeting, nodding at him.

Jasper Tudor, the new king's own uncle, straightened up.

"It is 'Her Grace the King's Mother' now," he corrected, referring to Margaret Beaufort, though his tone was not malicious or cruel.

Elizabeth smiled despite the fact that title ought to have been hers if only her sons had not been stripped of their legitimacies, an act which had led to so much chaos.

"Of course," she said finally.

"You are to be housed there, at Coldharbour," Jasper Tudor continued, "until the wedding."

Lizzie looked from Jasper to her betrothed then, hoping to gauge from his expression how he felt about this match, the one he had promised to make years ago but, with it suddenly approaching, may no longer be what he wanted. His face, half cast in shadow, was neutral, his mouth a horizontal line, his forehead undisturbed.

Lizzie frowned. He was hard to read.

"When might that be?" Lizzie's mother asked, returning everyone's attention to her, "The wedding."

Jasper Tudor turned and extended a hand to another of the king's men, who handed him a rolled-up document.

"The king and his council have much to – put right before that may come to pass," Jasper said, presenting the scroll to Elizabeth. A loaded silence befell them as Elizabeth Woodville stared down at the document, only the occasional crackling of the fire in the corner providing some semblance of life in the still room. Everyone present knew what insult that paper beheld – the Act Parliament had passed that saw Lizzie and her siblings be declared bastards. Finally, Elizabeth tore her eyes away from it and met Jasper Tudor's gaze, unwilling to take it. He tucked the unread scroll into his breast pocket.

"The question of illegitimacy aside," Jasper went on, "we must also apply for a papal dispensation due to the matter of consanguinity. Among other things. You will all be made very comfortable at Coldharbour until all affairs are taken care of."

Elizabeth nodded briskly and smiled, reminding everyone of what a beauty she had once been, before grief and heartache had etched away at her looks.

"Very well," she concluded, clearly pleased with the meeting.

Lizzie shifted her regard from Jasper to the king once more, continuing eager to assess the man who would soon be her husband.

Beneath the black riding clothes and gold-stitched cloak, she could tell he had a slender but well-built and strong body. His face was clean-shaven but marked with what appeared to be a scar on his chin. His nose was straight and narrow, and his eyes appeared a blue-grey. She froze then as he slid his gaze to meet hers, catching her unawares and holding her stare.

Grey, she thought. *Definitely grey.*

She swallowed hard, conscious suddenly that he had been observing her just as she had been observing him. And she found herself hoping – *for the future of England, of course!* – that he liked what he saw.

October 1485

In the two months since Henry Tudor's victory on the field, he had quickly learned that kingship was a testing ordeal. Especially given that he had claimed a broken country.

"For over half a century, no monarch has passed on the crown of England without turmoil," Jasper Tudor reminded his nephew one morning as they made their way to the council chambers, "building a new dynasty will be a battle!"

Henry, clad in a black velvet jacket and matching hose, scoffed at his uncle's choice of words, "And here I thought my fighting days were behind me."

"With kingship come rumours," Jasper said, trying to reassure him, "Every monarch has been subject to gossip."

"This goes beyond trivial gossip, Jasper," Henry replied, quietening his voice slightly as they crossed paths with a handful of courtiers, "The rumours that the York Princes are still alive grow louder each day! I fear I will be fighting *this* battle for the rest of my life!"

Following his victory at Bosworth, Henry had sensed a general acceptance of him as England's new monarch. The people had welcomed him into London, the air had been thick with cheers and joy. But whispers about Edward IV's imprisoned sons having survived and escaped the Tower had quickly begun to circulate.

And, though he didn't believe it to be true, the potential for pretenders cropping up to overthrow him was a threat he could not ignore. The first year of a new monarch's reign was uncertain, and he knew that, hidden in the shadows, there were still those of the Plantagenet line and Yorkist supporters who would seek to oppose him.

"What of the other Plantagenet boy?" the king asked as they turned a corner and approached the council chambers. The guards at either side of the door bowed their heads, but the king was too riled by the rumours of the lost princes to take notice.

"Edward Plantagenet," Jasper sighed, "Known as Teddy. As a boy of the Yorkist line he is, of course, a threat. His sister, Maggie, too. But the girl can be married off to a loyal Lancastrian in due time."

Henry clenched his jaw and nodded. He had hoped to avoid unnecessary arrests, but following the heavy gossip surrounding the survival of the Princes in the Tower, he had to root out any other potential dangers. Leaving the Plantagenet boy to roam free could cost him his throne and his head.

"Have the boy housed in the Tower," the king ordered bleakly, ashamed by the words, "We need to keep an eye on him. At least until the rumours about the other two boys have died down."

Coldharbour, London

The morning damp clung to the walls at Coldharbour, and Lizzie was warming herself by the fire in her chambers. Her cousin Maggie Plantagenet sat beside her, staring dreamily at the flames.

Maggie had recently been appointed as one of Lizzie's ladies-in-waiting following her brother Teddy's instalment in the Tower of London. At twelve years old – and a Yorkist Princess – Maggie needed to be kept close, so that she may not be potentially used in a plot to overthrow the new Lancastrian king.

"How much longer will we have to be here, Lizzie?" Maggie asked as she continued to stare pensively into the hearth.

Lizzie opened her mouth to answer, but on second thought, stopped herself and shook her head, "I do not know."

"You ought not to fret, Lizzie," came a voice from behind them. They turned towards the sound and saw Lizzie's sister, Cecily, approaching from the adjacent room. She stood before them now, a playful smile on her lips, "It'll cause you to wrinkle," and she gently tapped the space between Lizzie's eyebrows.

Lizzie swatted Cecily's hand away and gave her a look, "Wrinkles are the least of my worries."

"You shouldn't be worried at all," Cecily reiterated, "The Lady Margaret Beaufort has assured me all is going well at court."

Lizzie's frown returned and Maggie dropped her head.

"The king's mother has told you so?" Lizzie asked, having been unaware of her sister and future-mother-in-law's kinship.

Cecily nodded, stepping around them to warm her hands by the fire, "We pray together sometimes."

Just then, as if summoned by the mere mention of her name, Margaret Beaufort entered, the rhythmic padding of her soft footsteps alerting them of her approach.

All eyes turned to the lady, and Lizzie took in her pious attire.

She had heard of the lady's tragic history, Margaret and her mother Elizabeth having been acquainted for as long as Lizzie could recall. The king's mother had even been Elizabeth's lady-in-waiting at one point during her queenship.

As a descendant of Edward III, Margaret – like Lizzie herself – would've had a claim to the throne of England if only she had been born male. Instead, Margaret had been married off at just twelve years old to her first husband, Edmund Tudor, who had been twice her age at the time. Though a union at such a young age wasn't necessarily unheard of, it *had* been expected of Edmund to wait at least two years until Margaret was of age to consummate the marriage. But eyebrows were soon raised when, upon dying in battle, Edmund Tudor had left behind a very distraught, and very pregnant wife. And just a few months later – at the tender age of thirteen – the young widow had gone into labour. From what Lizzie had heard it had been a truly shocking incident, Margaret almost dying during the arduous process, her underdeveloped body having been ill-prepared for childbirth. She had never borne another baby since – though she had married thrice thereafter – and had instead dedicated her life to her one son and to God.

And yet despite all that, one did not pity Margaret Beaufort. For she was as strong and resilient as any woman could be.

"I bring excellent news!" Margaret beamed then as she addressed Lizzie, "The king has successfully repealed the *Titulus Regius* passed by Parliament. Yours and your sisters' legitimacies have been restored!"

Lizzie exhaled a breath so great and sudden that her chest ached with it. But it was an ache she welcomed, for it replaced the powerful churning in her stomach. At least momentarily.

"Thank you, Your Grace," Lizzie said sincerely, looking to her sister, who raised her eyebrows as if to say, *See?*

"And what of the wedding?" Lizzie said then, "Preparations must be made soon –"

"The pope has not yet authorised your union," Margaret interrupted, sounding irked, though not with Lizzie, "We are still awaiting the dispensation."

"The matter of consanguinity will not be a problem," Cecily assured with a shake of her head, "The pope will grant it."

Margaret nodded, "But until he does, we shall focus on other matters besides the wedding. The king's coronation, for instance."

Lizzie flinched, would they not be crowned together?

She only realised she had spoken the question aloud when the king's mother sighed.

"It is imperative that Henry displays himself to his people as their leader *ipso jure*," Margaret explained, "He must establish himself as king in his own right, without you by his side. He is the monarch, after all. You are to be his consort."

"Of course," Lizzie said with a nod, pretending this delay did not worry her.

When in truth, it had awakened the serpent in her belly once again.

What if the wars will never end?

Chapter 2

<u>30th October 1485</u>
<u>Westminster Abbey, London</u>

As the crowning ceremony approached, London was humming with anticipation.

Despite the time of year, the day marked for Henry Tudor's coronation was surprisingly clear, with naught but a wisp of white cloud in the grey-blue sky, and not even a hint of a breeze. The streets were cleaned and strewn with fragrant herbs and rose petals – both red and white. The path from the Tower of London to Westminster was adorned with tapestries and banners displaying the new king's arms: the Royal Arms of England and France, with the Welsh Dragon and the Greyhound of Richmond as supporters.

Crowds had gathered to catch a glimpse of the new king as he travelled by barge to Westminster, their elation reverberating from all sides, followed by cheers from those who spotted him during his approach.

Dressed in a crimson velvet gown and a fur-lined robe, Henry breathed in deeply to calm his nerves as the barge bobbed along the river, the motion – or rather, the entire event itself – making him feel slightly queasy.

For Henry knew that despite the cheers, there was danger lurking in the shadows, and whispers of the princes' survival churning in people's mouths.

"He is crowned," Lizzie said as she sat by the fire, embroidering alongside her mother and Maggie, "And quite without me."
Maggie did not reply and pretended to be engrossed in her needlework. But Elizabeth offered her eldest daughter a smile.

"He has not forgotten the agreement," she assured her daughter, though Lizzie had begun to wonder if her mother even believed her own words anymore.

"His actions to restore your legitimacy is proof enough of that," Elizabeth went on, "The gifts he sends emphasise it further."
Lizzie looked over at the bolts of fine fabrics Henry Tudor – *nay, Henry VII* – had sent her just two days prior. Ten yards of crimson velvet and six yards of russet damask, as well as sixty-four timbers of ermine. They had already ordered for dresses to be made from the materials, and there would even be enough for new robes for Lizzie's younger sisters, Anne, Catherine and Bridget.

"I think it will cheer you to know the king is to grace us with his presence on the morrow," Elizabeth added with a smile, "The king's mother received a message earlier. He requests a private audience with his bride."
Maggie's head snapped up abruptly, then gasped as she pricked herself with the needle. She sucked on the tip of her finger.

"The king is coming here?" she asked, her eyes wide and shining with fear.
Elizabeth nodded, "Don't fret, Maggie," she assured, taking the twelve-year-old's hand, "You are safe. As a girl, your Plantagenet blood is no threat to the king."
Maggie smiled tightly, then returned her attention back to her needlework, but not before Lizzie saw a flash of sadness.

"Maggie…" Lizzie whispered gently, hoping to soothe her cousin, who had been deeply distraught by her younger brother's arrest, "Teddy will not come into any harm if I can help it."

Maggie looked up and met her gaze, "But can you?" she challenged gently, "Help it?"

Lizzie opened her mouth to answer but her mother cut her off.

"Teddy is safe in the Tower," Elizabeth said, "He is lodged in one of the best rooms and taken good care of. The king has only placed him there for his own protection, so that he may not be used as a figurehead for rebellions. It is for the good of the realm that he be kept out of the reach of those who would use him and put him in direct danger."

Lizzie and Maggie shared a look, both of them hearing the irony in Elizabeth's words, for had her own two boys not been put in the Tower for the exact same reason?

And yet they knew what Elizabeth said was true, though it didn't hurt Maggie any less to hear it.

Imagining her little brother imprisoned in the Tower, alone and afraid, made Maggie's heart hurt. And no matter how pragmatically she thought about it, she only wished she could protect Teddy in a way that meant he did not need to be locked up. But what protection could she ever offer him?

"If the weather remains dry tomorrow," Elizabeth said then, steering the conversation back to a brighter topic, "perhaps you and the king could enjoy a walk in the gardens."

But Lizzie, saddened to see her cousin so blue, ignored her mother and leaned forward, "Perhaps, when the king and I are better acquainted, I could speak for Teddy."

Maggie gasped in surprise, "Oh, would you?" she asked excitedly.

Lizzie nodded, "I can try."

"You must not get your hopes up, Maggie," Elizabeth interjected, "The king needs to establish himself. Having Teddy run free would be detrimental to us all."

"He is but a boy," Maggie argued timidly, her mousy features pinched.

"He is a Yorkist heir," Elizabeth corrected, "Need I remind you what happened to *my* Yorkist heirs? And that at the hand of another Yorkist king, their own uncle! You are lucky to have your brother still. And thanks to a Lancastrian king at that."

It was no secret that Elizabeth believed her sons to be dead.

It was what any logical person thought, though Lizzie had heard the rumour mill churning of late. Whispers of their escape taunting hope into people's hearts.

But not Lizzie or her mother. They had long ago resigned themselves to the most probable reality.

The boys were dead. And people should allow them to rest in peace.

Maggie's eyes shone with panic at Elizabeth's statement, but she turned a smiling face to Lizzie.

"I hope you and the king will find common ground," she said with youthful optimism, "Perhaps even affection. If it means my brother might be kept from harm, I hope you two fall madly in love."

"I am not marrying for love, Maggie," Lizzie countered gently, a little laugh brightening the sombre mood, "This is but a political union. I am marrying for England. But at the very least I pray for a friendship, one built on mutual understanding. I will speak for Teddy if I can, Maggie. And I give you my word that while I am queen, no harm will come to him."

The following day, Lizzie was standing in front of her full-length mirror and smoothing down her blue silk dress, eagerly awaiting her betrothed's arrival, when Cecily knocked on the open door.

"Am I interrupting?" she asked rhetorically.

Lizzie shook her head before taking a seat at the window overlooking the courtyard.

Cecily sat beside her and followed her gaze to the gate where the king would soon pass through.

"Are you nervous?" Cecily asked quietly.

The sisters' eyes met, Lizzie looking suddenly like the younger of the two, her expression one of apprehension and doubt, "I hear talk that he plans to wed me in the new year."

Cecily nodded, "I have heard the same," she admitted, "My Lady the King's Mother has mentioned January more than once."

January. She could wait until then, Lizzie thought. She only hoped nothing would happen until then that would change the king's mind.

Cecily, sensing her sister's unease, touched her gently by the hand, "What is it?"

Lizzie turned away from the window and offered Cecily a small smile.

"I fear it will not work," she confessed in a tired whisper, "This union of the Houses. I fear the nobles will not see it as enough. If it happens at all…"

Cecily furrowed her dark blonde eyebrows, and Lizzie thought then how much Cecily looked like their father.

"Why wouldn't it?" Cecily asked.

Before Lizzie could reply, a call from outside alerted them of the king's arrival. With a gasp, Lizzie turned to once again look out the window just as Henry and his King's Guard trotted though the open gate. And she couldn't help but notice how majestic he looked on his black courser.

"Well," Cecily said when Lizzie didn't immediately stand, a mischievous grin playing on her lips, "Either you meet him, or I will."

Moments later, with her dress flowing behind her in her haste, Lizzie entered the courtyard to meet the king, curtsying elegantly as he dismounted.

"Your Grace," she said in greeting, looking him in the eyes when she rose.

He looked well, she thought, somehow taller since last she saw him – which was of course ludicrous, a man of twenty-nine did not suddenly grow overnight. She decided his recent coronation must have had something to do with it, God's anointing no doubt causing him to stand with more confidence.

"Princess," he replied, bowing his head.

She thought she noticed his lips quirking into a brief smile, but before she could be sure, it had vanished.

"Shall we take a walk?" he asked, glancing up to gauge the weather.

Lizzie followed his gaze and, glimpsing an overcast but dry sky, nodded in reply.

They strolled towards Coldharbour's garden, which was not large nor of flamboyant display like that of the royal gardens at Greenwich or Westminster. Yet, within its crooked stone walls, there breathed a strange elegance among the evergreens.

Upon entering, Lizzie felt herself relax a little, its privacy offering her a moment of reprieve from the pressures of the outside world. She breathed in the crisp air, allowing it to fill her lungs, then risked a look at the king beside her.

He was walking slowly, with his hands clasped behind his back. Corporeally, he appeared at ease, though his expression suggested differently.

"You seem far away, my lord," Lizzie noted, breaking the silence that had stretched between them.

Henry turned slightly to her, managing a small smile, "My thoughts are never far from matters of the realm. There is much that needs my constant attention."

Lizzie looked away, "And you being here is a distraction?"

Henry shook his head, "No," he replied calmly, "Quite the contrary. It is a necessity."

It was the first they had conversed beyond pleasantries, and yet his response made Lizzie's stomach drop. It seemed she was no more than a stepping stone to him. A box that needed ticking off on a list.

But she was nothing if not her mother's daughter, so she applied a smile to her lips, displaying strength when she felt none.

"You smile, my lady," Henry stated, "Why?"

She shrugged, "Why not? I am to be Queen, after all."

She had tried not to make her statement sound like a question, but her nervousness betrayed her, her tone lifting slightly at the end.

"If I will have you," he said in jest, one side of his mouth twitching into a half smirk.

But Lizzie was too nervous to catch the wit in his remark, and the serpent in her stomach hissed into life.

"Who else would you select if you had the choice?"

Henry chuckled under his breath, "Choice?" he echoed, raising one auburn eyebrow, "We do not have that luxury, you and I, Princess. But…your sister Cecily was also offered to me."

Lizzie's throat constricted, but she forced herself to look indifferent.

"Then why did you not ask for *her* to join you today?"

He looked at Lizzie sideways, then reached across the gap between them and tucked a stray lock of golden hair back underneath her hood.

"I prefer a fairer lady."

Lizzie thought of Cecily's dark blond mane and frowned, but then she noticed a crinkle at the corners of his lips.

"You jest," she summarised, looking away as they turned the corner of the garden and walked towards a skeletal quince tree.

Henry chuckled, "I admire a woman who can find humour within the burden."

"Admiration is easy," Lizzie countered, raising her chin, not in the least amused, "It is trust that comes slowly. Especially when so much depends on our union."

"You mean peace. Unity. Legacy."

"Among other things."

"Such trifling matters," Henry quipped, flashing a smile. Again, with the humour.

Lizzie stopped then, causing Henry to do the same. He looked over his shoulder at her, his eyebrows raised in question.

"I mean truth, too," she said, her tone serious. They had no time for jesting, and she, no patience for it. England needed security, and Lizzie needed answers.

"I wonder if you think of me as the woman who will be your wife," she said, "or merely as a symbol to secure your position as king. If joining our Houses and ending the fighting is even your wish…"

Henry opened his mouth to speak, then paused. It seemed she cared not for lightening the mood. And he was surprised to realise he respected her for it. There really was more to his betrothed than a meek princess.

He took a step towards her, his easy grin replaced with a more thoughtful expression.

"I would be a fool to deny what our union symbolises, and how important it is," he admitted deliberately, measuring each word, "And I am not blind to the strength you have clearly inherited from your mother, or of the grace you carry so easily, Elizabeth, the grace of your father."

Lizzie blinked up at him, pleased with his reply. Perhaps he did mean to stay faithful to his word.

"Lizzie," she offered, an olive branch, a chance at amity, "Call me Lizzie."

He nodded, "England needs *you* by my side, Lizzie. And no other. I thought you knew that. I thought you knew that *I* knew that."

A rain drop fell onto her shoulder then, and she looked up to find the clouds had turned a shade that promised imminent rain. But she was not yet ready to end their private moment, when she had only just glimpsed a peek at his truth.

"Then let us speak plainly to one another now," she said, "Without humour, but with honesty and a little kindness. We are strangers still. But…perhaps not for long?"
Henry nodded slowly, understanding finally that she needed to hear him say it: that he would make her his wife and put an end to England's bloodshed.

"I have a design I would like to show you," he said, reaching into his breast pocket and pulling out a small, rolled up piece of paper. He handed it to her, squinting up at the sky to assess the paper's safety in the light drizzle. Lizzie unrolled it carefully, examining the single element on its white background.

"A rose?"

"The Tudor Rose," Henry corrected, pointing at its details with a slender finger, "The red of Lancaster, joined with the white of York. One rose, united. No more division. It is my new emblem." Lizzie looked up at him, warmth blooming in her chest like the very flower he had designed, and when his grey eyes met hers, she felt a genuine smile tugging on her lips.

"May December pass swiftly," he said soberly, as he looked into her eyes, "and let January come in peace."
And with a shaky exhale, the rattling viper in Lizzie's belly ceased.

Part 2

Death is not the tragedy, but a life unlived is

Chapter 3

20th September 1486
St. Swithun's Priory, Winchester

It was just eight months after Henry VII and Queen Elizabeth of York's wedding night, but their baby was eager to be born.

"Push, Your Highness, push!"

The Queen of England didn't know which of her half dozen midwives was instructing her, their voices and faces all having moulded into one in the chaos.

Half sitting, half crouching on the birthing chair, Lizzie could hardly focus, not on her breathing, not on the midwives' instructions, not on her body's instincts. Dread was coursing through her, and one single thought continued to taunt her: the baby was coming too soon…

"Mother!" she cried, squeezing Elizabeth Woodville's hand tightly as another contraction ripped through her.

Elizabeth mopped her daughter's sweat-beaded brow, swept the damp locks of golden hair from her face.

Lizzie could do this, Elizabeth had no doubt. She came from a long line of strong and fertile women, Elizabeth herself having birthed twelve children, and her mother before her, Jacquetta, a staggering fourteen.

But the fear of childbirth was unavoidable all the same: the gritted breathing, the sharp scent of iron in the air; there was no knowing if it would end in unmatched joy or soul-shattering grief.

Especially, when the child decided to enter the world a month before its time.

"You can do this, Lizzie," Elizabeth mumbled lovingly to her daughter, a twenty-one-year-old Queen of England, but still a little girl in her mother's eyes.

Lizzie's bulging belly tightened then, alerting her of another contraction. Clenching her teeth, she squeezed her eyes shut tightly and bore down, letting out a deep and throaty groan as she pushed her baby out.

"Yes!" one of the many midwives breathed cheerfully, "I have it!"

A sigh of the purest relief escaped the queen, and she let her head fall onto the back of the wooden birthing chair as the midwife stood, wrapping the child in a blanket.

Lizzie's ears rang as blood pumped around her body and she tried to catch her breath.

It was over. She had survived the most daunting moment of her life. All was well. All would be well.

The young queen felt her mother's presence move away from her then, and it was as if the air went suddenly cold. She opened her eyes and searched the room for her, only then noticing the loaded silence that had befallen them.

"What – what's wrong?" Lizzie stammered, her throat raw.

A midwife was holding a covered bundle in her arms – or rather, *over* one of her arms – and gently rubbing its back as the others stood pointlessly around her, watching her work with troubled eyes.

"What are you doing?" Lizzie cried, tears pricking her eyes, "Mother?"

But Elizabeth ignored her daughter, instead taking the bundle from the midwife and rubbing the baby's back more firmly.

Lizzie could not take her eyes off the scene in front of her, and a pained noise escaped her when the blanket fell slightly off the child to reveal a beautiful tuft of auburn hair. She held her breath, each moment stretching on as though time had stood still.

And then – finally – the most delicious newborn cry echoed through the palace.

King Henry and his mother stayed awake all night when news had come that Lizzie had gone into labour.

Margaret sat silently reading the bible by candlelight while Henry paced up and down before the fire in the great hall, chewing on a thumb nail, unable to console his mind of his worries.

Henry *needed* this birth to be successful; for his reign may very well hang in the balance.

He had thought that marrying the York Princess would've been enough to squash any lingering opposers' doubts as to his sovereignty. But a hum of unease continued in the air, and only months after their union, an assassination attempt had quickly opened Henry's eyes to the truth: there would always be those who would contest a king, no matter how well he married, or how staunchly he stood for peace.

In hindsight, it had been a relatively pitiful attempt on his life, the minor rebellion coming to nothing once the instigator, Francis Lovell, had fled York. And Henry, wanting to show strength in the face of danger, had pardoned the involved rebels.

But underneath the stoic persona, he had been shaken, and ever since, he'd prayed daily for the arrival of a healthy child. For what a king needed to protect his crown was a strong dynasty – a nursery full of heirs. Only *that* would quell people's minds. Which was why, when Lizzie had announced her pregnancy mere weeks after their wedding, Henry had ordered for his court poet, Bernard André, to write of the king and queen's joy throughout the country. So that all of England would know that his son and heir would soon be underway.

A messenger entered the great hall then, his hurried footsteps echoing against the walls of the vast, empty room.

Margaret closed her bible with a gentle *thump*, standing to receive the news, ready to either congratulate or console her son. But a sigh of relief escaped her when the messenger began to speak with a smile on his young face, evoking good news. *Nay,* she corrected herself as she listened, *It was perfect news!*

"A boy?" King Henry repeated with a disbelieving exhale. The messenger nodded cheerfully, congratulating the king on the delivery of his heir.

"How is the child?" Margaret asked, her face beaming with grandmotherly delight, "He was born a little early, does he fare well?"

"I am told the physicians deemed the prince strong and healthy."

Margaret Beaufort pressed her bible to her chest and chuckled cheerfully at the information, thanking God under her breath.

"Take me to her," Henry said then, clapping the messenger on the shoulder and steering him towards the door.

A gasp escaped his mother, "You cannot see her, my son," she argued gently, "She has not yet been churched by a priest. She must be purified before –"

"Don't, Mother," the king interrupted her, casting a swift glance over his shoulder as he continued out the door, "Lizzie is my wife and she has just delivered my heir, how can that be judged impure."

Margaret Beaufort stopped in her tracks, leaving the king to do as he pleased. As Henry's mother – albeit an absent one for most of his life, Henry having grown up largely in exile – her only task now was to guide him. What he did with her higher wisdom was his decision, and she had given in to this reality many years ago. But it hurt nonetheless when he dismissed her, as though she was no more than a trivial old woman. She wondered sometimes if her son forgot that she was only thirteen years his senior. Not old by any stretch of the imagination.

Moments later, the king cautiously entered the queen's birthing chambers, searching the dark rooms for his queen. The air was thick with the scent of sweat and blood. Not unlike the smell of a battlefield, Henry thought. Though, on the battlefield, at least, there was an underlying current of fresh air. Here, in this woman's version of war, there was no such crisp reprieve, the midwives believing that a birthing chamber must emulate a woman's womb: dark, quiet, and sealed off of any sunlight.

Henry shuddered as he stepped further into the rooms and saw Lizzie lying in the four-poster bed with beeswax candles dotted all around her, setting an eerie mood. She lay on her back in the centre of the bed, her hair in soft waves around her, her eyes closed and her chest gently rising and falling. If he didn't already know that she and the child were well, Henry would think this a sombre picture indeed.

He felt suddenly like he shouldn't disturb her. No doubt she had been through a difficult ordeal, one he would never fully comprehend. And yet he could not stop from looking at her.

"Your Highness," a woman's voice whispered from the shadows then, a midwife appearing before him holding a bundle, "Do you wish to meet your son?"

The king did not need to answer, the woman handing him the newborn.

Henry took him in his hands, one cradling the tiny body, the other the head.

Holding the sleeping child before him, quite unsure how to move, the midwife stepped closer and, sensing his naivety, showed the king how to properly hold the babe against his chest, laying him in the crook of the king's elbow.

He thanked the woman, only allowing himself to focus on his son's face – the only part of him that was visible from within the white swaddling – when he felt certain the babe was secure in his grasp.

Hoping to get a better view of his child, as well as to avoid disturbing the queen as she slept, Henry walked carefully into the other room, where a fire glowed brightly.

"So much depends on you, sweet boy," Henry muttered, as he glanced lovingly down at his firstborn son, the child who would – God willing – one day become King of England.

Henry bent down and gently kissed the top of the baby's head, breathing in his honeyed scent and suddenly feeling a mixture of both great relief at his safe arrival, and overwhelming guilt for the pressure put upon the child already, only moments after his arrival into the world.

The midwife, who had followed him, looked down at the new prince with a smile, "He is beautiful."

Henry nodded, taking in his son's small nose, his red eyebrows, the soft slits where his eyes remained closed as he slept, the long eyelashes that sprouted from them.

"He is," the king agreed, his throat cracking with emotions he had never felt before: a visceral need to protect, an instinctive love that seemed to radiate from deep within his bones.

He *had* to ensure this child's survival. England's future depended on it.

The baby squirmed then, like a caterpillar in its cocoon, and the midwife offered her arms.

"He will want feeding," she explained, as another woman emerged from the gloom, rosy-cheeked and large breasted.

"Of course," Henry said, handing over his son, feeling strangely torn to be parted from him, though they had only just met.

"Henry?" his wife's voice called softly from the bedroom behind him then, groggy from sleep and exhaustion.

He turned in a flash, his heart soaring. Though they were still virtual strangers, he felt a glowing sense of pride for his wife's achievement, and he couldn't wait to make his gratitude clear.

"My queen," he breathed, kneeling beside her bed and taking her hand in his.

"Have you met him?" she whispered tiredly, "Have you seen him?"

Tears welled in her eyes, but Henry knew they were tears of delight.

He nodded, his auburn hair falling from where he kept it tucked behind his ears, "He is a wonder."

Lizzie reached up to touch the stray strand, "He has your colouring," she remarked, and Henry recalled the splash of red on the babe's tiny head, his red eyebrows.

The royal couple looked into each other's eyes then, the moment needing no words.

Their joy, their sense of achievement and relief – it was palpable. For this child was not just their heir, but the physical embodiment of the future they had promised England.

Half York, half Lancaster, this boy would lead the country further into peace when they were dead and buried.

October 1486

Lizzie's time with her son was painfully brief, for as the heir apparent to the throne, Prince Arthur was swiftly established in his royal nursery away from the court – as was custom – to ensure he commenced life with as much potential to thrive as possible.

"He will be well looked after by Lady Darcy," Henry said, assuring Lizzie for the third time since their departure, "as you well know. She was your own governess, after all."

Lizzie nodded solemnly, looking out of the window as the carriage gently swayed. She knew Henry was right, and believed that Arthur was in safe hands, but the ache of her separation from her baby was raw nonetheless.

"It is difficult, all the same," Lizzie explained, "Only weeks ago, he was a part of me. And now I shan't see him until –"

Tears sprung to her eyes and choked her into silence. She turned to look out the window again, her eyes unseeing, her throat tight.

In the few months since their wedding, she and Henry had formed a strong foundation of friendship and trust, but she still did not feel completely at ease to be vulnerable around him.

"You may visit him for the New Year," Henry reassured her helplessly, knowing nothing would lift Lizzie's spirits.

All he could do was be a pillar of strength for her. And he was surprised in that moment to realise that he *wanted* to be that for her.

"His household is well established," Henry went on after a while, "Lady Darcy, Catherine Gibbons, the rockers, the wetnurses…they are all verified and well paid. They are devoted to you as their Yorkist Rose, and nobody will have access to him that isn't loyal to us."

Lizzie smiled weakly at Henry as they rocked lightly in the carriage, though it was nothing she didn't already know. Henry smiled back briefly, but quickly broke eye contact with her after a moment, when he felt warmth starting to rise up his neck.

Ever since the birth of their son, Henry had begun to see Lizzie in a different light.

He had always admired her, had told her as much only months after their first meeting. He had the utmost respect for her as his wife and queen. But they had married for the sake of England and duty, not for the sake of love, and while that had been completely acceptable to Henry to begin with, he had recently begun to hope for more.

<u>January 1487</u>
<u>Sheen Palace, London</u>

Upon their return to London, Henry had decided that he would court his wife, regardless that she was already his by law.

He'd laughed to himself at the notion: courting his wife *after* she was already his. Who would do that?

A man who was falling in love.

The answer came to him like an arrow to the chest, and he could not deny it, for the evidence was right there in the flush of his neck when she looked at him, in the need to comfort her when she was down. And in the spirit of leaving his fighting days behind him, Henry decided he would not resist his own emotions.

He began by organising private dinners, and walks in the gardens despite the growing winter chill. And in response, Lizzie showed an equal willingness to spend more time with him, too, which only spurred Henry on all the more. They would speak of their childhoods, their hopes, their fears, no topic ever feeling too private, too out of bounds. They grew to understand each other on a deeper level, beyond that of their superficial compatibility. And though they did not always see eye to eye on trivial matters – *That is quite* clearly *the call of a goose, my lord. Not a duck! –* their core beliefs aligned almost exactly.

"How about a game of Triomphe, my lady?" the king said now, pulling out Lizzie's chair at the games table in the great hall.

It was almost four months since their first courtly rendezvous following the birth of their son, and though they had often ventured out into the garden for leisurely walks over the Christmastide – wrapped in furs and wool – January had brought with it a frightful snowstorm, causing the court to have to entertain themselves indoors until it cleared. But Henry would not allow mere weather to deter him from pursuing his wife.

They played in relative silence, stealing glances at one another over the lip of their cards and playing footsie underneath the table, smiling knowingly. But despite their easy flirtation, Lizzie would not be distracted, surprising Henry with a winning hand again and again, and by the end of their third game, he was left speechless.

"Don't underestimate me, Henry," Lizzie laughed, that gentle song Henry had grown to adore of late.

Their eyes met across the games table then, neither of them speaking beyond what was being said with their regard.

It was a simple setting, same as their entire courtship had been in the past few months. There were no grand gestures, no lavish events. Just the two of them, out on modest walks, sharing easy conversation. And yet, without even having known it, it was all Henry had ever wanted.

After a lifetime of uncertainty, hiding in exile, and fighting in battles, Henry cherished this simpler side of life with Lizzie. Not the kingship, the ruling, the pressure. But these peaceful moments they shared when it was just the two of them.

Henry felt an odd – but not unpleasant – tightness gripping around his heart at this realisation, making it somehow harder for him to breathe.

But in that moment, as her blue eyes blinked quietly back at him, he didn't care. For if falling in love meant suffocating, Henry would gladly forfeit air.

Chapter 4

<u>May 1487</u>
<u>Farnham Palace, Surrey</u>

Unbeknownst to little Arthur, it seemed not everyone was willing to give in to peace, for King Henry's rule was once again under fire. This time not by a mere rumour, or a feeble assassination attempt, but with the appearance of a Yorkist pretender.

"Who is he?" Arthur's nursemaid, Catherine Gibbons, asked his governess the Lady Darcy as they watched the rocker lull baby Arthur to sleep by the fireplace.

"They are saying he is Teddy Plantagenet, the Yorkist heir."
Catherine frowned, "I thought he was housed in the Tower?"
Lady Darcy shrugged, "It likely isn't the true Plantagenet boy. But I hear he is gaining support in Ireland and that Burgundy is backing this pretender with an army."

"An army!?" Catherine exclaimed, to which the little prince whined sleepily from across the room, and the rocker looked up sharply, casting them a stare that said to either keep it down or leave.
Lady Darcy touched Catherine Gibbons on the arm and jerked her head to the side, "Come."
They shuffled out the door and walked slowly along the candlelit hallway.

"What will this mean for the prince?" Catherine asked, a frown worrying her brows.
Lady Darcy sighed, "Nothing. King Henry will no doubt squash whatever this is. He surely has a plan. The army supplied by the Duchess of Burgundy cannot possibly be large enough to overthrow our king."

The nursemaid swallowed hard and shook her head, "The Duchess of Burgundy is our queen's own aunt. How can she think to support an attack on her own flesh and blood?"

"She is still grieving her late brother, King Richard III's, death," Lady Darcy explained, able to understand the Duchess' actions, though she didn't agree with them, "As a Yorkist herself she clearly does not wish for our king to continue on the throne. So much so she would rather back a false Plantagenet boy above her own niece and great-nephew, our Arthur."

Catherine shuddered, though the winter chill had been banished with the coming summer.

"God bless us during these uncertain times," she said, "I had truly hoped that England's domestic battles would be a thing of the past."

<u>Westminster, London</u>

"There is no need for panic," King Henry VII uttered calmly as he sat upon his throne in the great hall, addressing his wife and council, and Lizzie's shoulders relaxed unconsciously at his words.

She had grown to take comfort in his serene demeanour, just as she knew he had grown to take comfort in her steadfastness.

But at a time such as this, where not only her husband was at risk but now also her child, she wished she had something more tangible to hold onto than merely his serenity, some hard, physical knowledge that, yes, they would come out of this unscathed.

"The boy is but a puppet," the king continued, "He is not a genuine threat. As you well know, we *have* the real Teddy."

"But the people do not know that," his Uncle Jasper countered, "Give the common folk a boy of around the same age and they will believe him to be Teddy if they are told as much. He has gained much support already and it is growing at an alarming speed."

Some of the council members standing before him nodded their heads, but Henry already had an answer.

"It is easily rectifiable, my lords," he said, exuding composure, "All we have to do is dispel this pretender by showing the masses that this rebellion is based on a lie."

"How will we do that?" Lizzie asked, unable to keep quiet.

Henry fixed her with those steady grey eyes, like two stones at the bottom of a lake – secure, stable, unfaltering. Like no matter what happened all around him, he would remain consistent.

But she knew that – at least in part – it was all a show. That, in truth and behind closed doors, Henry often fretted about hidden threats, ghosts of the past that might come back to haunt him. And this scenario was exactly the type of thing she knew he feared.

"I believe I have something in mind."

Just as the pretender had been paraded around the streets of Ireland to gain support, so was the real Teddy Plantagenet paraded around the streets of London to counteract the false boy's backing.

Teddy, who was just eleven years old, struggled to understand why he was suddenly granted his freedom for a few hours a day, and why he was allowed to travel through the city in a royal carriage. But Teddy embraced the moment, waving to people as he passed them by, and throwing them coins – just as King Henry VII had ordered him to.

Teddy enjoyed seeing the people's faces light up at the sight of him, enjoyed watching them scramble on top of each other to catch the coin he had thrown into the dusty road. He wondered if it meant he would be allowed to return to his former life, if it meant the end of his imprisonment.

But after a week of tasting freedom, Teddy Plantagenet was returned to his cell in the Tower, too dangerous to be allowed to leave, too innocent to be left unsupervised.

<u>16th June 1487</u>
<u>East Stoke, Nottinghamshire</u>

Showing the people that the real Teddy Plantagenet Earl of Warwick was in fact in London and under the king's authority prevented the rebellion from growing any further in numbers, but it wasn't enough to foil the attack completely. And King Henry met his opposers head on, just as King Richard had faced him but two years prior.

Although Henry was certain this day would not mark the end of his reign.

Henry flew his new banners featuring a red and white rose, the new emblem of the Tudors representing a merged Lancaster and York. He had designed it as his new crest, to further show the world that Henry Tudor wished to rule the country in unified peace.

And yet it *still* hadn't been enough for some.

He shook his head.

Sitting tall on his black warhorse, his crown placed firmly on his head, the king overlooked the field where the battle would take place, alleviated – though not surprised – by the rebels' clear disadvantage. Their numbers were not enough to make him worry.

The Yorkist rebels were around eight-thousand men, mainly poorly armed Irish troops and German mercenaries. King Henry's army, in contrast, totalled at around fifteen thousand men, formed by two separate groups led by the king himself and Lord Strange, the king's stepbrother.

Henry had hoped that by simply displaying to the rebels how vastly outnumbered they were would be enough to deter them.

He did not wish for any more bloodshed in the name of the crown. Not when he had offered the country eternal peace, and especially not when the would-be supplanter was a fraud.

But, against Henry's inclination, the rebels engaged in battle nonetheless, and the king had no choice but to respond.

It was a bloody skirmish, one with heavy casualties, particularly among the poorly armoured Irish. They were shot through by English archers only moments after the first battle cry had sounded out. And the king could do nothing but watch the people be slaughtered.

Towards the end of the battle, the remaining Yorkist army began to flee towards the River Trent, and Henry watched from the top of the hill as they were chased down by his larger army, to be captured or killed.

Afterwards, the River Trent ran red with the rebels' blood, and Henry's chest panged with remorse.

So much life was unnecessarily lost, when the entire conflict could've been avoided.

Sheen Palace, London

"The false boy has been captured," Lizzie informed her mother, Cecily and Maggie as they strolled through the palace gardens, "He is to be pardoned by Henry as a gesture of clemency and given a job in the royal kitchens. His real name is Lambert Simnel."

Lizzie inhaled deeply, allowing the summer air to fill her chest before she broke the rest of the news.

"This rebellion has shaken Henry. And me," she admitted, casting a quick glance at her sister and cousin, "It is no longer safe to assume the Yorkists are at peace with Henry as their king simply because I am by his side. It is not enough, it seems, to deter rebellion."

Her mother nodded, already knowing of what she spoke.

"Which is why the king, his council and I have arranged for your marriages," Lizzie said, looking at the two young women walking beside her.

Cecily gasped, an eager smile brightening her face, "Who? Who have you chosen for me?"

Lizzie relaxed slightly to see her sister so keen to be married again. After her first marriage to a lesser noble two years prior – forced onto her by King Richard – had been successfully annulled by Henry, Lizzie hadn't been sure how Cecily would react to being married off again. She smiled to see her sister so pleased.

"We have chosen 1st Viscount John Welles for you, Cecily."

Cecily's eyes widened, "The Lady Margaret Beaufort's half-brother?"

Lizzie nodded and Cecily squealed with delight, turning to their mother and chattering excitedly about how she would soon be a Viscountess.

But Maggie looked less enthused, her eyes shining with angst.

"Will I have to move away?" she asked Lizzie, "Will I be able to keep visiting Teddy in the Tower?"

Lizzie pressed her lips together, her stomach twisting to think of the positions she and Henry have had to put her cousins in to ensure their own son's safety. But in the world they lived in, it was either *their* wellbeing, or *Arthur's*. And to Lizzie, her son would always come first.

"I don't know, Maggie," Lizzie admitted, her chest heavy, "But I am told your betrothed is a kind man. His name is Richard Pole. He is Henry's first cousin, and he is loyal to him. Like us, he is eager for peace between the houses, which is what really matters."

"Do you think," Maggie said in between sniffles, "that – maybe the king would consider releasing Teddy now?"

Cecily turned back to rejoin their conversation and took Maggie's hand, "Maybe one day…when – when the country is more settled…"

Lizzie nodded and smiled tightly when Maggie looked at her.

But Elizabeth, older and wiser, sighed, turning her face to the summer sky, "Don't get your hopes up, Maggie," she said, "The safest place for your brother to remain is in the Tower. There he cannot be plucked up to spearhead another rebellion. In there, he will at least get to live."

Lizzie nodded in agreement at her mother's words, resolved to put the matter to bed and focus on the victory at hand. And yet, she couldn't help but think: If a life imprisoned was considered living, then surely death would be a kinder outcome.

Maggie and Cecily excused themselves then and headed indoors, Lizzie having no doubt that Cecily would be spending the next few hours talking wedding details.

"I hear talk of Arthur's betrothal has begun, too," Elizabeth added then, regaining her daughter's attention.

Lizzie frowned and glanced at her mother, "Arthur is too young to be betrothed," she dismissed, raising her chin defiantly as they walked.

But Elizabeth chuckled softly, looping her arm through her daughter's, intent on enjoying the rare moment of privacy she had with her before returning to her residence in Bermondsey Abbey.

"My dearest Lizzie," Elizabeth said sagely and with a hint of sadness, "Sons and daughters of a king are never too young to be betrothed."

Despite King Henry's external display of calm, the Simnel Rebellion had disturbed him, though he would never admit to it. Except, perhaps, to his wife.

"How is our son?" Henry asked Lizzie one evening as they dined in private in the King's Chambers. She had recently corresponded with Arthur's governess, the queen wanting to be as involved in their son's nursery as possible, though her duty was to be away from him at court.

"He is well, Henry," Lizzie beamed, pride warming her chest, just as the glowing hearth warmed the chambers, "Lady Darcy reports he has never once caught so much as a sniffle. He is strong."

Henry nodded, glad to hear it. A weak heir would not do.

"Has Parliament passed the Household Act?" his queen asked him then, leaning back to allow the servants to clear her plate. She thanked them with a smile.

"Not yet," he sighed, "But they will. We need it. To tighten security around the royal family is imperative. We cannot risk nobles drifting into opposition with my kingship. You know as well as anyone how that might end."

Lizzie nodded. Sometimes, she still couldn't believe that her own Uncle Richard had gone against his own flesh and blood to obtain power. But he had.

But did he have my brothers killed, *too?*

The thought popped into her head again, same as it did every time the topic was broached. And the reawakening of people's gossip following Lambert Simnel's impersonation of Teddy only fed Lizzie's lingering doubts.

"They are saying my brothers are still alive."

She whispered this as Henry held his cup up to be refilled, and she saw how his jaw tightened at her words. But she could not have withheld them any more than she could've withheld from exhaling, the long-dismissed topic having grown like a canker in her mind. His gaze flicked from her to the servant pouring his wine

"They have been saying that for years," he replied casually, like it meant nothing. He ran a hand through his auburn hair and tucked it behind his ears.

He had greyed a little since his victory at Bosworth, thin strands of silver having appeared at his temples. He was only thirty-one, but his short – yet tense – time as king was clearly taking its toll.

"Do you think there is any truth behind the rumours?" Lizzie asked, unsure as to whether she hoped for them to be true or not, her love for her brothers conflicting with her love for her child. For their survival could possibly mean the end of Arthur…

Henry looked at her from across the table with hard eyes, and Lizzie flinched slightly at his pained expression.

"Would you wish them to be true?" he asked wearily.

Lizzie swallowed hard, taken aback by the question, taken aback by her hesitation. But quickly enough, the flood of love she had for her son drowned out any lingering desire to ever see her brothers again. Though a pinch of remorse caused her heart to sink.

She raised her chin.

"I am a Tudor," she said, "My loyalty will always be to the family we have created, not to the one I have left behind."

She thought of young Teddy, alone and frightened in the Tower. He would likely never step foot outside those walls again. And – like with her brothers' fates – the incompatible swirl of emotions that came with that fact churned her stomach. The same way oil and water did not mix.

Chapter 5

<u>March 1489</u>
<u>Farnham Palace, Surrey</u>

Prince Arthur was not yet three years old when he first heard about the girl who would one day be his wife.

"Be – beetroot?" the little prince said, trying to repeat the strange new word.

His governess, the Lady Darcy, who Arthur loved more than anyone in all the world – apart from maybe his favourite nursemaid, Catherine – chuckled warmly.

"Betrothed, my prince," she said, nudging his chin with her finger, "one day, God willing, you and the princess will be wed."

He nodded as though he understood, knowing it was expected of him, and Lady Darcy straightened up to continue talking to his nursemaids.

Arthur tuned their chatter out after that, his young mind still stuck on what he had just been told, trying to decipher it.

What did she mean, 'be wed'? Was it like a spider's web?

He looked up at the gossiping women, a frown etched between his auburn brows when the rust-red plumage of a chaffinch flying past them caught his attention.

A smile broke out on his face and he sprang up to chase it, not yet in full control of his movements.

A chorus of cooing noises sounded from behind him, and he knew without looking back that his nursemaids were watching him play.

"The *Infanta* Catalina de Aragon is said to be very beautiful," Margaret Beaufort said, clutching her rosary beads as she stood before her son in the council chamber, unable to hide her enthusiasm for this splendid match for the prince.

"She is the daughter of two powerful Catholic monarchs," Henry replied calmly, re-reading the documents in his hand, "*That* is what matters."

Lizzie, who sat beside her husband, offered her mother-in-law a smile, "I hear she is receiving the best education, given that Spain approves of female monarchs."

It was true. The Spanish princess' mother, Isabella de Castille, was the ruler of Castille in her own right, a Queen Regnant. As such, the queen's daughters all received a wider education beyond that of dancing, embroidery and languages, but also of politics, history, and battle tactics.

Lizzie thought briefly of how much war could have been avoided over the years had England been as forward thinking as Spain.

"With this Treaty of Medina del Campo," Margaret continued, shaking Lizzie from her thoughts, "Not only have we secured a strong marriage pact for our Arthur, but also provisions for equal trading rights between our two nations."

"And for defence from France, Lady Mother," Henry added as he signed a document and handed it to Jasper, who stood beside him, "That was a crucial detail of the treaty."

Margaret nodded and waited as her son and daughter-in-law stood and headed for the door. She held back to give them priority, but also to fall into step with Jasper.

She sighed contentedly once they had gained enough distance from the royal couple to speak privately, "I am relieved," she admitted, "This has surely just changed everything. Our Henry has officially gained international prestige with this treaty. If the rulers of Catholic Spain have agreed to betroth their princess of the blood to Arthur, then it solidifies Henry's standing as King of England. No royal would've betrothed their princess to a boy they did not see as the future king!" she brought her rosary beads to her lips and kissed them, "God is good!"

Jasper grunted in agreement.

Margaret looked at him and spotted that familiar crinkling of his eyes. Even with his bushy grey beard, she knew he was smiling.

"I am grateful to you, Jasper," she admitted then, feeling warmed by the new developments.

He made a sound of dismissal, but Margaret knew that he would want to hear it, "God is good, there is no doubt. But Henry would not have achieved this life had you not been by his side."

Jasper scratched at his chin self-consciously, then smoothed his short beard with the palm of his hand, "It was you who gifted England such a fine man, Margaret."

The king's mother breathed a laugh, "I birthed him and loved him from afar, yes. But it was you who shaped him into the man he is today."

They both directed their attention to Henry then, walking arm-in-arm with his queen as he looked adoringly down at her.

"Our boy is happy," Jasper observed, and Margaret nodded, tears welling in her eyes to see her son basking in the glory of his triumphs.

"He certainly is."

October 1489
Farnham Palace, Surrey

Thick, dark clouds had been gathering ominously over the palace all day, evening falling that much sooner due to their murky gloom, when dozens of bolts of fine cloth were delivered to Farnham at the order of the king.

"The king has plans for his heir, I take it?" Lady Darcy said as she watched each bolt be carried in by officers of the king's household.

None of them needed to answer, for what they carried over their shoulders was clearly for a grand occasion, fabrics of the best quality being quickly brought inside before the rain began to fall. Lady Darcy spotted white velvet, coloured silks, satin, black bogi, even fur of ermine. And along with the fabrics, a note from the king that ordered the prince's textile workers to make new gowns and tunics.

She smiled warmly at the king's household officers once they had successfully delivered every last bolt of fabric, then ushered them outside just in time to witness a jagged bolt of lightning in the distance.

"You'd best hurry back, gentlemen," she said, "Storm's coming," and she turned, the guards closing the doors behind them.

She entered the prince's royal apartments just as thunder rumbled lazily overhead.

"No doubt Arthur will soon receive his title," she said to Catherine Gibbons, who'd been keeping an eye on their ward while she received the delivery, "He is to have a whole new wardrobe."

At the sound of his name, Arthur looked up from where he'd been playing with his wooden toys, a bright smile conquering his face at Lady Darcy's return.

"Come now, my prince," Lady Darcy said, reaching a hand towards him, "Time to clean our hands before supper."

He stood and took her hand, the two of them heading to a basin by the fire.

Arthur dipped his hands in the lukewarm rosewater, taking special care not to splash and make a mess – he had learned early on in life that to make a mess was not princely.

Lady Darcy dried his hands with a cloth then, and Arthur looked up at her with the purest regard, joy bubbling in his chest just to be near her.

And then he said something that would alter his perspective of the world forever.

"Thank you, lady mother."

Lady Darcy stiffened, a slight frown twitching between her eyebrows when she bent down, "What did you say?"

Arthur swallowed, looking from Lady Darcy to Catherine sitting on a chair nearby.

They were both looking at him with the same confused expression.

Had he said something wrong?

Was he in trouble?

"He called you 'lady mother'," Catherine said, and Lady Darcy nodded.

"Yes, I thought so."

She laughed then, a tender sound, and yet it suddenly did not comfort Arthur like it once used to.

"I am not your mother, little prince," she said, straightening up and throwing a look of amusement to Arthur's nursemaid.

Arthur looked from Lady Darcy to his favourite nursemaid, his cheeks growing hot with humiliation and feeling oddly off-balance on his feet.

"You are not my mothers?" he asked, his voice cracking and his chin wobbling.

Lady Darcy clicked her tongue as though that were obvious and led him to the dinner table.

"Of course not, Arthur," Lady Darcy said. Did he sense a hint of annoyance in her tone?

"Catherine and I are but your caretakers," she went on, "You know who your mother and father are."

Arthur followed her gaze up to the portraits on the wall, where the two strangers he knew as 'the king' and 'the queen' stared back at him.

He nodded, because he felt like he should.

"They are your parents," Lady Darcy explained, "You must never call me or Catherine or anyone 'lady mother' again, unless it's your actual lady mother. Do you understand?"

He nodded again, though his throat began to tighten and his vision began to blur with hot tears.

Lightning flashed in through the windows then, followed quickly by a loud thunderclap right above them, and Arthur took that opportunity to scurry from the dinner table and onto his nursemaid's plump lap, where he had always felt safest.

"Now, now, my prince," Catherine chuckled as she patted his head gently, his face pressed into her lap, "It is but thunder."

He held onto her tightly as another thunderclap sounded, even allowing a little sniffle to escape while they believed him to be afraid of the storm.

"Is God angry?" he asked after a moment, his little voice muffled against Catherine's dress. Though what he'd really wanted to ask was: *Have I been bad?*

Catherine stroked his wispy auburn hair, but the answer came from the Lady Darcy.

"It is but a storm," she said, "It will soon pass."

Arthur peeked out from Catherine's lap to see Lady Darcy standing by the window watching the gale. She seemed completely at ease, utterly unperturbed by the chaos outside the palace walls or indeed the chaos within them.

Was she not aware of how Arthur's world had just tilted?

He watched her for a moment longer, then hid his tear-stained face in Catherine's lap once again. Though it, too, no longer felt as it had once done.

And the little prince suddenly thought how wrong his governess was.

The following morning, dawn broke with the cheery chirping of birds and the fresh scent of wet earth and grass. The sun rose in a golden glow, beams of light shining in through the windows of Arthur's nursery. It was like the world was born anew, washed clean by the storm.

But within the stone walls of Farnham Palace, the air now felt sullied and warped, like time moved differently to Arthur – slower, quieter – as though he were in some kind of dream.

He had woken early, before even the first glimpse of dawn, and settled himself on the woollen rug by his bed, his wooden soldiers and horses strewn before him. His little hand, still soft and dimpled at the knuckles with youth, clutched at one of the soldiers now and he brought it close to his face.

The sound of the door opening made Arthur look up from his toys, and two servants entered the room.

Lady Darcy, who was sitting by the fireplace, her head bent at an angle as she quietly read her bible, ignored them. But Arthur observed the two young women as they arranged his breakfast on the table, whispering to one another and giggling under their breaths, never once even glancing in his direction, as though he didn't exist.

After what he had learned the previous night, it all made so much sense now.

"Come now, sweet boy," Lady Darcy called to him then, closing the bible on her lap and putting it aside, "Time to break your fast."

She held out her hand to him and he rose up to accept it, letting her lead him to the basin in the corner of his room. His governess wiped his hands with the rosewater. It was cold, and he flinched slightly but did not resist.

She sat him before his breakfast and urged him to eat, before taking a seat in front of him and applying a smile to her face. Arthur realised now how forced it looked, how unnatural, and he wondered if his true mother would look at him with a purer kind of love. He tried to remember the last time he had seen her – or his father – and realised he couldn't, his courtly appearances being but an annual occurrence every Christmastide. And their visits to his nursery were few and far between. It made his chest ache.

"Now, Arthur," Lady Darcy said with a breathy sigh, "We have received news from court."

The boy looked up, "From my lord father?" he asked, feeling the fog in his mind lifting slightly.

Lady Darcy nodded, pulling a note out from her sleeve. She handed it to the prince, though he could not yet read. But Arthur was simply happy to stare at the king's seal at the bottom, proof that even if he didn't quite remember his father, his father remembered him.

"Soon," Lady Darcy said, explaining what was written on the letter, "You shall receive a great honour. And, if we're lucky, we might be in London when your mother the queen has her baby."

Arthur's pale eyebrows shot up, "A baby?" he asked.

He hadn't even known there was to be another baby. Where did parents even get one? Was he to be replaced? His little hands started sweating.

Lady Darcy chuckled softly, a sound he had once cherished, but now it was just jarring, "Yes, a new baby! You are to be a big brother, and soon you will share your nursery with your new sibling."

<u>28th November 1489</u>
<u>Westminster Palace, London</u>

A damp mist clung to the castle walls as dawn broke over the horizon and the Queen of England gave birth to her second child, three years after the first.

King Henry, unable to be with her, stood by the open window of his bedchambers staring out into the ethereal land, aware of its mystical appearance but utterly blind to it, for his soul was with her, even if his body was not.

He knew nothing of childbirth, only that it could be as dangerous as it could be fulfilling, depending on the outcome. He knew that it was a woman's very own battleground, and that to be nonchalant about it was unwise.

He thought of Lizzie now, of the pain she must be enduring, of the trepidation she must be feeling, not only for herself but for their unborn baby, and – even – for Arthur. For, to go through such an ordeal when one was already a parent invoked a fresh kind of fear: the fear of abandoning the child you had already grown to love if something were to go wrong.

Henry exhaled deeply at the parade of terrifying thoughts marching through his head. He had to clear his mind. Nothing good would come from thinking the worst.

So he thought of better things. Of the way Lizzie's smile lit up her entire face, the way her eyes shone when she spoke of Arthur…how her skin felt on his fingertips, the way her mouth tasted when they made love.

They had conceived Arthur on their wedding night. Henry knew this because it had been the one and only time they had been intimate in the months following their wedding. But after Arthur's birth, when Henry and Lizzie's companionship had evolved into something deeper, the royal couple had not wasted any more time, and they'd explored their newfound affection for one another at any chance they got.

They'd conceived again quickly, and Henry had lavished Lizzie with gifts and attention, making sure she had anything her heart desired.

And yet, despite their joy to soon welcome another child, it was a testing time following Lizzie's happy announcement. For she and Henry had not yet extinguished the burning desire that had recently sparked between them; but being with child, Lizzie could no longer engage in any activity that might put the pregnancy at risk.

The young couple had had to make do with little more than passionate kissing, but the desire to touch her and hold her had almost been too much for Henry to bear, and he felt as though he were some lovestruck teenager again!

His physicians had urged him to take a mistress in the interim, to satisfy his needs and maintain his health. But Henry had paid them no heed, for he was not a foolish man. He knew what he had with Lizzie was special, sacred; and he would not endanger it for a night of meaningless release with another.

Not only would he never dare to disrespect his wife – his *queen* – in such a way, but Henry also knew that to sire potential bastards would only cause trouble in the long run. The line of succession needed to be absolute! To create possible usurpers to his own heir would not only be reckless, but it could also potentially renew the wars he had promised to end.

But more than anything, Henry had no wish to bed another woman.

He'd had his fair share of encounters in his youth – as any healthy man would – but when he was with Lizzie, it felt different. It felt right. As if, no matter what, his destiny – even above being King of England – had always been to be hers.

He wondered then, as he continued to stare dreamily out the window, if *this* was what poets wrote about: this feeling of being both grounded and floating all at once, of being finally whole despite having found your other half in someone else…

The sound of someone clearing their throat returned Henry to the present, dispersing his beautifully tortured thoughts of what he had found with Lizzie, and how it may all be dashed if she were to perish in childbirth.

He turned around swiftly.

"News, Your Grace," the young boy said, bowing his head, "The queen has successfully delivered a princess."

Henry's face lit up, the heaviness in his chest evaporating in an instant, "And she is well? The queen, how is the queen?"

"Very well, I am told," the boy said, "Resting."

The king grinned and slapped the messenger on the back as he headed out the door, his previous woes immediately forgotten.

"Alert the country!" he ordered as he made his way out the door and through the palace, "Ring the bells! Set off fireworks! I have a daughter! I have a daughter!"

29th November 1489
Westminster Palace, London

It was a time for celebrations, and not just for the birth of England's new princess – named Margaret, after her grandmother.

Arthur Tudor, now a big brother at the age of three, was to receive a great honour, befitting his status as the king's heir apparent. Just the previous day, the city had been alive with cannon fire to announce another royal birth, Londoners cheering for their monarch's good fortune. And now, in the great hall of Westminster Palace, the people had gathered to witness yet another historic event, courtiers and common folk alike having crammed themselves inside, murmuring amongst themselves in anticipation.

Tapestries emblazoned with the Tudor Rose draped the stone walls and a grand dais had been erected beneath the narrow, arched windows, its velvet canopy trimmed in gold. At its centre, clad in robes of deep scarlet and ermine, the young Prince Arthur sat with regal poise well beyond his years. He didn't swing his little legs, or sing songs underneath his breath. He didn't tug at his clothing, or bend his head all the way back to observe the intricate ceilings that always fascinated him. He wanted to, his little boy energy begging to be released. But Arthur had been carefully instructed how to sit and how to behave. And as the son of the king, he would do just that.

The ceremony began with a procession and Arthur raised his chin, relaxing his shoulders and looking ahead just so. Heralds in tabards bearing the royal arms entered first, followed by lords of the King's Council, and finally the king himself.

Arthur almost grinned at the sight of his father, who he hadn't seen in almost a year. But his father's serious expression reminded Arthur that he needed to remain composed, so the young boy pursed his lips and furrowed his brows. Anything to keep the smile off his face.

The king looked majestic and strong, Arthur thought, just as he hoped to one day be.

A hush fell over the great hall as the Archbishop of Canterbury approached the dais and Arthur watched with astonishment as the oldest man he had ever seen parted his dry lips and raised a shaky hand.

"By the grace of Almighty God," the archbishop called, "and at the will of His Highness, Prince Arthur, son of our sovereign lord, King Henry VII, is this day created and invested as Prince of Wales, rightful heir to the crown of England and guardian of peace to the Welsh lands."

He placed a mantle of cloth of gold lined in azure upon Arthur's little shoulders, and held a circlet of gold adorned with fleur-de-lis over his head, high up for all to see.

The choir sang a hymn, their voices echoing delicately through the hall, and a cannon thundered from the palace walls, causing Arthur to flinch. He forced his hands to remain at his sides, though he wanted to cover his ears against the loud *bangs!*

"God save the Prince of Wales!" the assembled crowd cheered when the sounds of the cannon subsided.

Prince Arthur knew that it was the moment he was to stand and bow low to his father, but the weight of the mantle was crushing him down. He wriggled it about on his shoulders, his face creased into a scowl of concentration, then he hopped off his seat and straightened up. He was suddenly sweating, and he thought how he would be glad when this day was over.

"God save the Prince of Wales!" the mass called again. Arthur, feeling suddenly overwhelmed, searched for his father's face in the crowd. Spotting him, he attempted to copy his father's austere expression, only to notice a hint of a smile on his lips. Arthur relaxed slightly then and allowed himself to grin, flashing all of his baby teeth. The throng of people cooed, delighted by the tender moment, by the boy's innocence, his purity.

Then, as he knew he was expected to, Arthur bent at the waist, bowing as low as he could without toppling forward by the weight that was that day placed upon his shoulders.

Chapter 6

January 1490
Farnham Palace, Surrey

When Arthur's baby sister Margaret joined his nursery at Farnham Palace, he had been overjoyed.

At last, he would live with someone who was family!

But when the newborn baby was brought to Farnham and set up with the silver crib that had once been his, in the baby room that had once been his, and with the nursemaids that had once been only his, Arthur wasn't sure what to make of it.

But, he thought after a spell, he didn't mind sharing. After all, he no longer needed any of that, since he was a big boy and no longer a baby.

Arthur was excited to spend time with his baby sister, his mind already reeling off all the fun things they could do. He couldn't wait to play with her, talk to her, teach her things.

But upon visiting her every morning before his lessons, Arthur soon realised that not only could she not play; she could not even move.

"Why is she wrapped up so tightly, Lady Darcy?" Arthur asked his governess – who was now also Princess Margaret's governess.

Baby Margaret was lying on her back at the centre of the crib, her entire body wrapped tightly with linens, buckles holding her arms and legs tightly in place.

"You were wrapped this way, too," she replied, "Babies are kept swaddled this way, their arms and legs straightened, to make sure they grow properly. She will be wrapped this way until she is nine months old."

"Nine months! But…" Arthur spluttered, suddenly realising babies were no fun at all.

He looked down at the pink newborn, frustrated with her futility. But he left his disappointment unspoken. For what could he even say that would make his sister grow up faster?

He retreated to his chambers then, feeling deflated.

<u>November 1490</u>

"Ah-ta! Ah-ta!" Princess Margaret babbled excitedly, when her four-year-old brother entered the room, a wide grin on his face and a wooden toy in his hand.

He hurried towards her, his baby sister, his best friend, and lifted her into his arms, nearly toppling over.

"You weigh as much as my pony!" Arthur teased, tickling underneath her chubby chin.

Margaret squealed with delight, her arms flapping excitedly at her sides.

Arthur put her gently back down and handed her the toy he had brought, then sat down in front of her. He watched as Margaret played, their governess sitting in the corner reading her bible and the servants hovering around unnoticed. He sang to her and told her stories, as he did every day when he visited, excited to build their connection in any way he could. She was still too young to do all the fun things Arthur had initially imagined he would do with a sibling. Climbing trees, exploring the secret passageways in the palace, searching for worms, those were all things a one-year-old could not do without supervision. And what fun would it be if the Lady Darcy came along with them? She most likely wouldn't approve anyhow.

But Arthur was happy to wait for Margaret to grow up, her presence giving him great comfort to know that he would no longer go through life alone.

Sadly however, those images were never to be, for not long after Princess Margaret's first year, Arthur's household changes would make it so that he had little to no time for pleasure.

<u>January 1491</u>

   As Arthur developed, so did his household, which was now of a much more formal structure than ever before.

Though the prince was still but four-years-old, King Henry had wanted for his heir to commence his kingly training earlier than was custom, in order to prepare his son to rule in case anything were to happen to him.

Where Arthur had once been surrounded by only female attendants in his babyhood, over the following few months the young prince had begun to notice that many familiar faces were being replaced by men. At first, the strangers had merely watched him silently as he played with his wooden toys. They would wordlessly take notes on pieces of parchment, scribbling furiously when he selected the archer over the knight, or if he sang to himself.

It had felt sinister, unnerving. And after a few days, he asked his governess what their purpose was.

   "They are simply observing your development to inform the king of your progress," she said, dismissing the young boy's concerns with a wave of her hand.

He nodded his head as though he understood, watching quietly as Lady Darcy returned her attention to his baby sister.

Arthur felt strangely transparent from then on. As though all his thoughts and feelings were visible to these watching men.

And one thing was made perfectly clear to the young boy: his childhood was coming to an end.

"Another lap, Your Grace," John Almor ordered, calling over the top of the horse's loud trot.

Arthur nodded once, then jerked the heels of his boots into his pony's sides.

John Almor, a man in his mid-thirties and a veteran of the king's hall, was one of the main military resources of the royal household. He had recently been appointed as Prince Arthur's first sergeant-of-arms and called upon by his king to safeguard the prince, as part of his changing education. Almor's role included a broad range of responsibilities, such as vetting of visitors and servants, and setting the watch. He was, in layman's terms, the prince's bodyguard.

"You mustn't push him too hard, he is but four," said the Lady Darcy, who had wandered down from the palace to observe her former ward.

She smiled. Arthur had always possessed an elegant talent for horse riding, thanks to the queen's master of horse Sir Robert Coton, who had trained him from babyhood. But Almor seemed to be working the prince excessively, and though Lady Darcy's responsibility over the prince had expired, she still cared for the young boy's wellbeing.

Almor sighed, "He is no longer your concern," he replied.

He could see Darcy raising her chin in his peripheral vision.

"Whatever the king's decision," she said, "that boy will always be my concern."

Almor turned to face her, "Are you insinuating something?"

Darcy's expression said it all. She did not agree with how early the boy was being worked into adulthood.

"I am but reminding you of the boy's age. He has been installed with you men years earlier than is custom. Be gentle on him."

Lady Darcy walked away then, casting one last glance over her shoulder and smiling at the prince. Almor followed her gaze and noticed Arthur returning her smile.

Almor frowned, displeased by Darcy's unsolicited advice. He had his orders, and they did not involve being lenient on the boy. Prince Arthur trotted towards him then, breathing heavily and squinting against the cloud of dust his pony had kicked up.

There was a question on the boy's face, as well as sweat, dirt and exertion. He was tired. He'd had enough. No doubt his muscles ached.

But Almor would be damned before he allowed some woman to tell him how to raise a future king.

"Again!"

Chapter 7

May 1491
Sheen Palace, London

"What if my Uncle Richard didn't have my brothers killed? What if he helped them *escape*?"

The queen was trying to make sense of the most recent development, wherein a young man of supposedly striking resemblance to one of Lizzie's brothers, arrived in Ireland claiming to be one of the lost Yorkist princes.

Henry made a noise halfway between a scoff and a grunt of unease.

"The story is thin and implausible!" he retorted, sounding less sure than he had hoped.

"But not impossible," Lizzie countered in a loaded whisper, her eyes wide, her pale face taking on an ashen hue.

From his spot before the fire, Henry stared at her from over his shoulder, then down at her round middle, where another Tudor prince or princess was growing.

He had feared this very day since his victory at Bosworth Field. But now that it had finally come, Henry felt far more afraid than he had thought he would. For if *this* pretender was real, Henry's reign might have come to an end, and so might the lives of his children.

A single knock sounded then, followed by the hurried footsteps of several people, and Henry and Lizzie turned towards the commotion.

"It is said he arrived in Cork in Ireland wearing fine clothing, ready to be received as a claimant to the English throne," Margaret Beaufort said without greeting or curtsy, getting straight to the point. The men behind her, however, didn't dare not to bow their heads at their monarchs.

"He came from Portugal, so they say," Jasper Tudor added as he straightened up, receiving a letter from the king's trusted military commander, John de Vere 13th Earl of Oxford, and handing it to the king.

Henry scanned the document as Jasper continued to speak, "He was known as 'The White Rose' during his time in Portugal –"

"Oh, God," Lizzie muttered, pressing a hand to her mouth and turning away.

"Before that, he'd been in Flanders," Jasper continued, adding half-heartedly, "So they say."

"*Who* are 'they'?" Margaret Beaufort demanded, casting an angry glance at Jasper.

Henry looked up from the letter to find John de Vere clenching his jaw and his uncle Jasper swallowing hard before replying.

"Everyone."

<u>June 1491</u>
<u>Farnham Palace, Surrey</u>

King Henry VII installed no governor of noble rank for Arthur, for he had learned from Lizzie's father's mistakes that trusting the wrong noble, even one who was family, could lead to usurpation. And given the king's newest strain, it was imperative that Arthur be kept safe.

Instead, educated but low-born tutors were to provide the prince's teachings, men who the king could trust to remain loyal to the continuation of the Tudor dynasty above any other.

John Rede, a former headmaster of Winchester School became Arthur's tutor, and, unbeknownst of the tension building at his father's court in London, the prince enjoyed his lessons very much.

"Try again, Your Grace," the grey-haired man said, closing his eyes and breathing in deeply, "Take your time, *feel* the words."

With the book closed before him, Arthur cleared his throat and began to slowly recite the passage of Virgil's 'Aeneid'. This time, the Latin words flowed more gracefully, and his little shoulders relaxed to see Rede nodding along.

The prince enjoyed learning new things. He had developed a great appetite for languages and poetry, and he was indeed grateful for the opportunities which being the Prince of Wales granted him.

But sometimes, when the night was too dark, or the wind whispered eerily, Arthur would miss his former life, when he could still call out to the ladies who had raised him, and they would come running. Regardless that they were not his mothers, as he'd once thought, they had always consoled him when he'd needed it. And in hindsight, that was all that had mattered, for he had recently come to understand that not only those related by blood could feel like family.

He only wished he had realised it sooner.

The prince hardly ever saw them now, for they were far too busy to worry about him. Not only because of his little sister Margaret – who kept them on their toes with her furious and constant desire to explore the outdoors – but also for the royal family's newest addition.

Baby Henry had been born just seven days earlier, a second son to the King and Queen of England, and to their delight he had been born strong. With a mop of copper curls and a scream that could be heard through the thick stone walls, Arthur sometimes wondered how anyone on that side of the palace managed to sleep. But if the dark circles under the rockers' eyes was of any indication, it appeared they, in fact, did not.

"Enough for today, Your Grace," his tutor said then, shaking Arthur from his thoughts as he stood gingerly from his seat, "You will need to rest well tonight. Tomorrow you will begin learning how to manage servants and officials. You'll need to have some understanding of that skill before your move to Ludlow."

Arthur had heard talk of this move far too often of late for his liking, but he had never been outrightly *told* about it. Not that being informed would alter anything, Arthur thought. If his father had made plans for him, Arthur could do nothing but obey. He only hoped Ludlow wasn't too far away…

"Will Margaret and Henry be coming with me when I go?" the boy asked, a flicker of hope remaining in him, even though he had already asked his sergeant-of-arms, John Almor, that same question. But Almor wasn't one for tenderness, and he had simply shrugged in response, caring little about it.

Rede slid the book back into place on a shelf between two others, then turned to Arthur, "No, Your Grace," he said with some compassion in his voice, "To preside over the Prince's Council is reserved only for the Prince of Wales. It is an honour meant only for you."

Arthur nodded. Somewhere deep inside, he had already known that would be the answer.

"Yes," he said, trying to evoke some gratitude into his tone, "An honour."

He repeated the word, trying it out on his tongue like one would a sugared fruit. But upon sampling it in his mouth, he found that, like an unreliable orange, it tasted surprisingly sour.

January 1492
Greenwich Palace, London

"The boy didn't even speak English when he arrived in Ireland last year!" King Henry bellowed, throwing documents across the table. Some fell to the ground.

A servant emerged from the corner and gathered them up before placing them all on a neat pile on the table and melting back into the shadows.

"He is a pretender! It is impossible for him to be the queen's brother!"

The king's loyal supporter, John de Vere, stared pensively past the king and into the glowing hearth, "If it is indeed true that the boy did not speak English before now, then yes, it is highly unlikely he is the Yorkist Prince."

Henry exhaled sharply and ran a hand over his face.

He had aged significantly since obtaining the throne just seven years prior. Though he was but thirty-six, the Tudor king's hair had gone almost completely silver, and his cheeks had grown gaunt. Kingship was most certainly not for the weak.

"What do we do?" Henry asked, looking past de Vere as the rest of his council entered the great hall in their fur robes and sombre expressions.

"We make a treaty with France," said one of the older men.

Richard Foxe was Henry VII's Keeper of the Privy Seal, and his main role was to handle negotiations with other European powers. He had been a supporter of Henry's since before his rise to the throne, which, to the king, was firm proof of his loyalty.

"France has betrayed England time and time again in recent years!" Henry argued, "And their support of this *pretender*," he spat out the word, as though it tasted foul, "will not be forgiven."

"France was once your ally, Your Grace," Foxe said, reminding Henry of France's aid to fight King Richard III, "It was the dispute over the Duchy of Brittany following your ascension which caused tension between our two nations. If we promise to withdraw our troops from France in exchange that they abandon all support of the pretender, we may just succeed in squashing the boy."

Henry looked to his Uncle Jasper and de Vere, who were both nodding slowly in agreement as they digested Foxe's proposition.

"We know what France's support for another claimant to the throne could mean, Henry," Jasper said, his eyes flashing briefly with a memory of the past.

"But he is a *false* claimant," Henry countered, not yet fully convinced that making peace with France would be necessary, "I was a rightful Lancastrian heir. This boy is a nobody! A Flanders born commoner!"

"We do not know that for certain," de Vere added cautiously, raising one dark eyebrow at his king, "The rumour of the boy's lack of the English language is not enough proof to dismiss him. It may be but hearsay, a way of putting us off his scent. We mustn't become lax."

The king paced up and down then, before *tutting* angrily and moving away from the fire. He was sweating. This was almost too much to bear.

"Draw up the treaty," he said, glancing at Foxe, who bowed his head and turned to retreat.

"One more thing!" Henry called after him, raising his chin. He would take full advantage of a new treaty with France, "Make sure France knows we will not retreat merely for their promise to stop supporting the pretender. England requests monetary encouragement to cease our military presence there."

Foxe nodded, aware that it was but an attempt for the king to save face, "Yes, Your Grace."

"The boy does not frighten me," the king said to the remaining councilmembers then, tugging at his crimson silk jacket and tucking a strand of grey hair behind his ear, "If France wants peace, they will have to pay for it."

<u>July 1492</u>

While France and England discussed the terms of their peace treaty, the French King Charles VIII invited the York pretender to France, and Henry was furious at the disrespect.

"France is enjoying this," he muttered, pulling his bow string tauter than he should, then angrily releasing his arrow, "This game he plays will be the death of me."

Applause rang out to the king's right, the courtiers praising his shot. But Henry hardly noticed. He hadn't even stopped to check if his arrow had hit the mark.

His mother sighed beside him, "I am less concerned with France's support and more with the Duchess of Burgundy's."

The king shook his head and took another arrow from the quiver held by his groom, "Lizzie's aunt…"

Margaret nodded, "She supported Lambert Simnel's rebellion. I have no doubt she is supporting this pretender, too. She has probably been his secret protector for years already."

Henry released another arrow, this time watching as it pierced the straw target dead centre. The small crowd applauded him again.

"So, you do believe he is the real prince?" Henry asked, muttering under his breath, unable to look his mother in the eyes.

Margaret swallowed and gripped her rosary beads tightly in her hands.

"No," she said, though her voice cracked. Then she added in a whisper, "He cannot be."

Henry turned to her, ignoring the waiting crowd, "How can you be so sure?"

He stood but inches from his mother, searching her face. She stared back at him, her head tilted back against his six-foot height.

"God would not be so cruel as to give you the throne only to take it away again," she said, with such certainty in her voice that Henry almost believed her.

"God didn't *give* me the throne, Mother," he answered, ignoring her disparaging *tut* at what she no doubt believed to be blasphemy.

"I took the throne," Henry continued in a rash whisper, "I *took* it, fought for it, *killed* the previous king for it. But let's say you are right, Mother. Let's say God gave me the throne. Why wouldn't He take it from me thereafter? He did so to my predecessor, and his predecessor before him!"

"That was different," Margaret countered, looking swiftly side to side when she heard the crowd begin to murmur inquisitively, "The Yorks were all usurpers. They *murdered* our rightful King Henry VI in his sleep, while under *their* protection in the Tower!" Henry clicked his tongue in annoyance and ran a hand through his hair.

"*Every* king is a usurper to the one before in one way or another," he argued, "And if Burgundy gets their way, then this false prince – if he is indeed false – may very well succeed in usurping me!"

He thrust his bow at his groom's chest then, the boy staggering backwards. Then the king stormed off towards the palace, too irked to continue with his pastime, and leaving the courtiers to gossip and wonder what the king was so worked up about.

<u>Farnham Palace, Surrey</u>

Arthur found out about his third sibling's birth one morning over breakfast, when the child's arrival at Farnham was announced.

"Another baby?" he exclaimed brightly, eager to meet his new brother or sister, "Is it a boy or a girl?"

Arthur's tutor, John Rede, smiled kindly at him, fascinated to note that the young prince seemed completely unperturbed that he hadn't even known his mother was with child. For the moment, it appeared he continued young enough not to notice his isolation. And Rede wondered when that realisation would suddenly hit.

"Her name is Princess Elizabeth," Rede told him, watching Arthur closely for any sign of upset. But he was all smiles and awe.

"After my mother and hers," the young prince beamed, "When can I meet her?"

"You may meet her when she is settled in and you have mastered this poem, Your Grace," Rede replied, ready to return to his duty, "Now, start again from the beginning! I will have no more distractions."

Chapter 8

<u>October 1492</u>
<u>Greenwich Palace, London</u>

France's continued show of support for the false York Prince made Henry reach a decision. If France would not willingly agree to the peace treaty between their two nations in favour of ceasing support of the pretender, then Henry would have to force them.

"Until they sign the treaty, our troops will not be called back," Henry explained to Lizzie as his grooms fitted his armour, "But it is not enough for my men to merely be there. I have to apply some pressure for Charles VIII to yield."
Lizzie opened her mouth to speak but thought better of it. Nothing she could say would change her husband's mind. She stroked his cheek instead, the stubble prickling her palm.

"Do not engage in battle," she requested quietly, knowing that as king he would do as he pleased, but hoping that as her husband he would heed her warning.
Henry took her hand from his cheek and pressed a kiss to her palm, "With any luck, I won't have to."

In the king's absence, Henry VII appointed his six-year-old son as Keeper of England and King's Lieutenant, leaving Arthur in sole charge of the kingdom in his father's stead − in name, at least. And in order to do that, he had to be present at court.

"Of course, your father's council will reach the final decision on matters while the king is away," Arthur's head of security, John Almor, explained as they made their way to London, "You are far too young to understand or make valid decisions on your own."

"But it is excellent practice, all the same," Rede added cheerfully, winking at Arthur, his grey hair twitching in the breeze from the open carriage window.

Arthur smiled, though he cared little for the title or the practice, for he was simply glad to see his lady mother for the first time in two years.

Due to the queen's last two pregnancies being so close together, as well as the recent threat to the king's rule, Arthur hadn't been summoned to court since the Christmastide of 1490, and though he wasn't sure he even remembered his mother all that well, an innate wish to see her glowed warmly in his belly.

"Will my lady mother be on the council?" he asked.

Almor scoffed and looked out the window, but Rede leaned forward.

"No, my prince," he said, "As a woman, your mother's role is less political and more –"

"For the creation of heirs," Almor interjected.

"—Domestic," Rede continued, throwing a riled look at Almor. He turned back to Arthur, "You will see your mother, nonetheless. And you may discuss politics with her if you wish. Your mother is a very clever woman. She simply does not sit on the council."

At that, at least, Almor nodded in agreement.

As it turned out, all Arthur had to do to fulfil his role of Keeper of England, was to sit on a makeshift, miniature version of his father's throne each morning while the king's councilmen discussed foreign and internal matters.

Most of their talk went over the boy's head. In that regard, at least, Almor had been right – he was still far too young to understand of what they spoke. All the issues, the jargon, and even the many kings, queens, lords, dukes, earls mentioned, it was too much for his fledgling mind to comprehend. And though he knew he was but present for symbolic purposes, Arthur could feel his chest growing tighter as each day passed. Would he ever be fully prepared to rule an entire country?

But despite the anxiety brought on by the meetings, he enjoyed being at court.

Every evening, there was a banquet, a masquerade, or a ball, all of which he enjoyed immensely – for how couldn't he? They were all performances created especially for him! – and they were certainly a refreshing change from the humdrum evenings at Farnham, spent reading poetry or the bible with Rede or Almor. But even more delicious than the evening entertainments, was the time he was able to spend with his mother during the day, when council was finally adjourned.

"Tell me about your lessons, Arthur," his mother said one afternoon as they walked around the courtyard after Arthur had been dismissed from his morning duties, "Do you like your tutor?"

Arthur nodded, thinking of Rede's calm expression, his easy way of explaining, "I do, Lady Mother. He has taught me so much."

"And what is your favourite lesson?"

The young boy thought for a moment, considering what his lady mother would prefer to hear. If his father had asked him that same question, he might've answered horse riding or archery. He felt like his father would appreciate those answers above the truth. But his mother was gentle, like Lady Darcy and Catherine Gibbons, and Arthur felt at ease to speak honestly.

"Poetry," he said, taking his mother's hand as they walked past a handful of lords and ladies.

Lizzie smiled affectionately at her son, "I am told you are also skilled at archery? And dancing?"

The prince nodded, raising his chin proudly, "Almor says I am quite skilled. Like Father."

Lizzie laughed and put an arm around him as they walked.

"I have no doubt about that!" she said, pressing him to her side, "One day you will make an excellent king, my son."

They continued in silence for a while, relishing the sounds and smells of that rare dry October day, Arthur savouring the warmth of his mother's arm around his shoulders.

And he wished his time at court would never end.

Henry VII's trip to France was a success, and the Treaty of Étaples was signed without much resistance.

With this new alliance, England may have lost the Duchy of Burgundy to Charles VIII, but it was a small price to pay for King Henry's peace of mind. With this agreement between England and France, the pretender no longer had France's support, and the chance of him gaining enough troops to be of any real threat to Henry was slim.

Unless, Henry thought again and again on his return journey to England, *he was the* real *Prince Richard Duke of York...*

<u>November 1492</u>
<u>Farnham Palace, Surrey</u>

Arthur turned over a rock in the field behind the palace and gasped, the sight of a half-dozen grey worms wriggling back into the mud giving him a burst of awe.

He leaned back on his haunches and dropped his chin into his cupped hands, watching intently as the writhing creatures attempted to escape whatever danger they imagined he posed.

A raindrop fell onto Arthur's head then, a fat, wet *plop* sounding in his ears. He looked up. The oak tree he had settled under was not enough to contain the worsening rain.

"We should head back inside," said Almor, who stood by the tree trunk, "Wouldn't want to catch a cold."

Arthur ignored him, too focused was he on the worms' desperation to live, though he was no threat to them. But they didn't know that.

Unfortunately for Arthur, his father had returned to England just one month after he'd left, and Arthur had been sent back to Farnham, where his secluded life went on as though nothing had ever changed.

But something had changed.

During his time in London, where Arthur had gotten to bond with his mother, where he had danced at balls and attended jousts, he had come to realise that life at Farnham was barely a life at all.

Sure, he had his tutor, his security, his servants, even his siblings – albeit separated in the nursery wing – but he had no true connection with any of them. There were no festivities and very little play. His entire life revolved around learning and perfecting, preparing him for his *future*.

But what about his present? Arthur thought as he watched the worms attempt an escape.

Did his life *before* becoming king not matter?

Arthur poked one of the worms gently with the tip of his index finger then, and to his utter horror, he realised he *envied* those slimy creatures and their simple brains. They had only a handful of thoughts about life. Eat, sleep, survive, reproduce, die. It was very straightforward.

They were not tied down by obligation or duty, did not spend night after night agonising about their progress or what their fathers thought of them.

Arthur sighed, ashamed to feel envious of such a thoughtless creature when his life was so *good*.

But as he stood and nodded at Almor that they may return indoors, he wished he had a brain like the worms, because his was a cacophony of worries and fears.

Chapter 9

<u>April 1493</u>
<u>Ludlow Castle, Shropshire</u>

With each year that passed, Arthur's responsibility as the heir apparent grew, and shortly after his sixth year, the next step on his journey towards kingship was set in motion.

He was sent to Ludlow, as his father had planned for some time, in order to begin his higher princely education.

At Ludlow Castle, Arthur would preside over the Prince's Council – a miniature equivalent of the King's Council – and be set up with a makeshift court, one which resembled that of his father's, so that he may learn how to govern over a small court and council in preparation for his future as king.

And though this was – as his tutor had once told him – an honour, all Arthur knew was that he was henceforth to be even *more* secluded from his family.

"Will you visit us soon?" his sister Margaret had asked on the morning of his departure, her voice small and her eyes wet.

Arthur had pulled his mouth into what he had hoped looked like a smile, "I don't know," he'd answered honestly, taking her little hand in his and squeezing.

She'd hugged him then, fiercely, as though they had such a strong connection she couldn't bear to break it. But in truth, Arthur couldn't remember the last time they had played or laughed together. They had never gotten round to doing all the fun things he'd hoped to do when she was born. They hadn't climbed a tree together or explored the secret grounds. For he had always been too busy. But it seemed even despite that, Margaret still adored her big brother, and Arthur's heart had fluttered to realise it before he left. His two-year-old brother Henry and one-year-old sister Elizabeth, however, only blinked back at him in their nursemaid's arms. Siblings only in name.

As part of this change, there were several new faces appointed among Arthur's budding court, some of which included Sir Richard Pole and his wife, the queen's own cousin, Maggie.

Richard Pole was a loyal supporter and cousin to King Henry VII, and thanks to his unwavering devotion throughout the years, he had recently been appointed as Arthur's Chief Gentleman of the Privy Chamber, a most honourable and admirable position.

Prior to this role in the prince's household, Pole had been granted various offices in Wales, including Constable of Harlech and Montgomery Castles, and the High Sheriff of Merionethshire. His arranged marriage to Princess Maggie Plantagenet in 1487 had also helped in elevating his status among the court.

Initially, when he had first been informed of his impending nuptials to the young Plantagenet girl, the then twenty-five-year-old Richard had groaned internally; and had even hoped to repudiate the marriage. For Maggie – who had been fourteen at the time – was not only much younger than he, but also of much higher status, and he did not believe himself worthy of her. But one could not deny the king, and he had accepted the betrothal with quiet concurrence, promising Maggie on their wedding night that despite his lower status, he would always try to be a kind and respectful husband to her.

Six years had passed since that night, where he had forfeited his right as a husband to consummate the marriage and instead allowed the young woman to make her own decision as to when she would be ready. In the years that followed, they had formed a bond based on mutual respect and friendship, and though Richard did not think he and Maggie would ever be madly, passionately in love, he was proud of their development.

They had been married before God for four years, Richard having respectfully resigned himself to a loveless marriage, when, upon reaching her eighteenth year, Maggie finally allowed her husband to her bed. A son was born to them the following year in 1492 – who they named Henry, after the king – and Richard could finally safely say that he was happy beyond measure, though he had not chosen this particular path in life for himself.

And now, with this new opportunity, where he had been called upon by his king to safeguard the prince at Ludlow as part of his changing education, Pole couldn't be prouder of where his life had led to.

As Chief Gentleman of the Privy Chamber to Prince Arthur, Pole had a broad range of responsibilities, including making sure the prince's household ran smoothly. He would aid John Almor in making sure the prince was safe at all times.

And Pole was immeasurably grateful that he and his family would continue to be able to serve the Tudor House in the generation to come.

<u>May 1493</u>

"Gruffydd?" Arthur repeated with a frown, when the usher announced the young man.

He looked to Sir Richard Pole for confirmation, and he bobbed his head back at the prince.

Gruffydd straightened up from his bow and Arthur noticed a grin on his face, "Your Grace can call me Griffith, if you'd prefer," he said, his Welsh accent strong, "Griffith Rhys is the anglicised version of my name anyhow."

Arthur nodded, "Griffith," he said, testing it out and finding it suited the blonde boy just as well.

"Gruffydd ap Rhys is the son of Sir Rhys ap Thomas," Richard Pole explained, "who is the *de facto* ruler of most of south-west Wales, and who aided King Henry in his victory at Bosworth."

Griffith jutted out his chin with what Arthur thought was a hint of pride.

"Welcome to my court," Arthur said gallantly, as he'd been taught to.

Despite being eight years older than the prince, Gruffydd had been specifically chosen by the king for his heir's new household as part of a plan to surround Arthur with influential young men with powerful fathers. And given Gruffydd's father was one of the most powerful men in Wales, it made him the perfect choice for the prince's companion.

<u>August 1493</u>

"I bet my longbow that you will not defeat me," said the almost seven-year-old Arthur as he presented his bow to Griffith Rhys.

"That was a gift from your father," Griffith replied wide-eyed, "I wouldn't dream of taking it from you."

"You won't be taking it," Arthur corrected him with a playful smirk, "because you will not win."

Griffith raised his hands, showing his palms in mock surrender. Then he stepped back and allowed Arthur to take the first shot.

"Don't forget to breathe, Your Grace," Griffith reminded Arthur quietly, a chuckle in his voice.

Begrudgingly, Arthur exhaled and relaxed his shoulders.

He let loose the arrow and watched wide-eyed as it embedded itself just south of the red painted heart of the straw stag.

The prince turned to Griffith and handed him the longbow, "Beat that," he said, but Griffith could hear the faint hesitation in Arthur's voice. He knew that Griffith could do better than that if he wanted to. And the precious bow might soon be his.

The young man sighed and ran a hand through his dark blond hair, then shook the stray strands out of his eyes for good measure before taking his place. He lifted the bow and arrow, took aim. And shot the straw target on its rump.

"Ha!" Arthur exclaimed, practically jumping up and down with glee, "Hand over my longbow."

Griffith did, but not before tutting theatrically.

Though they were eight years apart in age, Griffith rather enjoyed spending time with the young prince. He was eloquent, thoughtful, and much more mature than Griffith had been at his age.

He felt sorry for the young prince sometimes, all too aware of how hard his tutors pushed him and how little time he got for leisure. And so, whenever he could, Griffith would try to instil some fun into Arthur's daily life. Hence the friendly archery match.

"That bow is too small for me anyhow," Griffith teased presently, pretending to sulk at his failure, though he had lost on purpose.

"What do you mean? This is a magnificent bow!" Arthur argued, running a hand lovingly along its limb, remembering how happy he felt to receive it.

Arthur looked up at his friend then, his eyes no longer playful or contrary but, to Griffith's surprise, apologetic.

"Would you like it?" the prince said, holding it out to Griffith.

The young man recoiled, "What? No, I couldn't!" He waved his hands in front of him and laughed nervously, "I was only jesting."

Arthur continued to look up at him, this young man who had been a stranger but some months ago and had since begun to feel more like a brother than his own ever had.

"I want you to have it," Arthur insisted, nodding encouragingly. And when Griffith started to refuse him again, he added, "I will take it as a personal insult if you do not."

Reluctantly, and feeling slightly guilty, Griffith accepted the generous gift.

"Thank you, Your Grace," he said, bowing his head, his blond waves flopping over his eyes again.

Arthur grinned, "It's about time you call me Arthur," and then, remembering Griffith's own choice of words when they first met, "if you'd prefer. It's the anglicised version."

Griffith laughed, his green eyes narrowing light-heartedly, "Do you know what 'anglicised' means?"
Arthur shrugged, "It's like 'easier', right?"
Griffith looked down at Arthur's excitable face. Sometimes he forgot just how young the prince actually was.
A call from the entrance of the castle caught the boys' attention then. It was time for Arthur to return to his studies.
  "Sure. It means easier," Griffith replied then, choosing not to correct the boy as they made their way inside.
Not everything, Griffith mused, needed to be a lesson.

Chapter 10

<u>1494</u>
<u>Greenwich Palace, London</u>

"Are you sure?" Lizzie whispered in the dark, the flickering light of the candle casting an eerie glow on her face.

Henry looked up from the note brought to him by one of his spies, one of many he had secretly installed in the noble's households following the Lambert Simnel rebellion. And now he was gladder than ever that he had.

"It is undeniable," he said, handing her the scrap of paper, "The very man who helped me achieve the crown has betrayed me."

Lizzie read the note, squinting to see it in the dim light.

If I were sure that the young man calling himself Richard Duke of York were really the son of King Edward IV, I would never fight against him.

Lizzie looked up at her husband, stunned by the treason she'd just read.

"There's nothing for it," she said, her voice shaking with rage, "Anyone with this mindset needs to be arrested."

Sir William Stanley, the brother of the king's own stepfather, and the very man whose support at the Battle of Bosworth had gained Henry the upper hand, was arrested and tried for treason against the crown, along with five other courtiers.

Stanley would be executed for his crimes, the others, depending on the evidence found against them, may very well face the same fate.

Stanley's arrest shook the court, not only for the fact that he was one of the king's own family – albeit of no blood relation – but also for the king's swiftness in dealing with the matter. But Henry could not allow for any chance of usurpation to take root in-house; he would rather cut out the seed of doubt before it had the chance to germinate. Regardless as to who had dared to plant it. To ignore it would mean he and Lizzie had learned nothing from her brothers' fates.

It was with that shocking development that Henry VII realised the pretender was not to be underestimated. For he was no longer only actively gathering support in Europe, but directly from within the English court. And Henry would not be supplanted the way his predecessor had been.

<u>July 1495</u>

Despite the pretender's lost support from William Stanley due to the man's arrest and execution, the pretender was not deterred, and he attempted to invade England with funding from Lizzie's own aunt, the Duchess of Burgundy. Just as Margaret Beaufort had expected.

"He continues to persist!" Henry hissed after the false York Prince landed with a force at Kent but was swiftly routed by local Tudor supporters.

Henry walked speedily through the hallways following a heated council meeting, his Uncle Jasper and Richard Foxe trying desperately to keep up, their aging bodies making them fall a few steps behind. At one point, Jasper had to stop entirely and press a hand to his chest before breathing in deeply and continuing behind his nephew.

"Even if he *is* the queen's brother," Henry grumbled angrily, "I swear I will see him dead!"

"He is not the queen's brother," Jasper added automatically, a sentence now so often repeated it was like a knee jerk response.

"We need but capture him, Your Highness, and then you may do as you wish with him," Foxe said, looking over his shoulder at Jasper, "I have heard word he has fled to Scotland."
Henry stiffened, Anglo-Scottish relations were already poor. England could not afford to have Scotland backing the pretender, too.

"How goes Parliament in regard to the Treason Act?" Henry asked, turning a corner and making eye contact with the guard standing sentry outside the queen's chambers. The guard bowed his head and made to open the queen's large wood doors.

"It shall be passed without issue, I hear," Foxe replied, he and Jasper slowing down, understanding as they approached the queen's rooms that their diplomatic talk was concluded.
Henry nodded but did not stop to look at them.

"Good," he said, "Leave me," and he strode into Lizzie's chambers, peeling his jacket from his shoulders as he entered.

Inside the queen's brightly lit chambers, Henry found his golden wife sitting prettily by the window, embroidering a Tudor Rose on one of his shirts, surrounded by her ladies.
He took a moment to simply look at her. The sun was shining through the open window and onto her blonde head, like a crown of the purest light. She looked ethereal, awash in a brilliant glow, shining brighter than the clearest diamond.
Lizzie, sensing his eyes on her, looked up and smiled, and a warmth burned inside him.

"Leave," he told her entourage, stepping out from where he stood in the shadows.
Her ladies quit the room in a flurry of satin and lace, whispering unintelligible gossip as they went.
Henry watched Lizzie, who continued to sit in the sunlight, smiling as she looked back down at her handywork.

"What brings you here, husband?" she said, though Henry was aware from the tilt of her head, the slight twitch of her fair eyebrows, that she knew.

He needed her, this gilded creature who he was lucky enough to call his wife. Sometimes he still did not know what he'd done to deserve her by his side.

A cloud moved before the sun then, momentarily blocking out its vibrancy without diminishing Lizzie – for she had her own radiance – but it was enough to dispel Henry's thoughts to the darkness that seemed to follow him constantly.

He frowned, "The pretender. He was not caught."

Lizzie's smile wavered briefly, but she quickly reapplied it and rose from her seat by the window, leaving her embroidery behind.

"But he was made to flee?" she asked, already knowing the answer.

Henry nodded and allowed her to take him by the hand and lead him through to the other room.

"I only wish I knew if he were your –"

Lizzie interrupted him by pressing a hand gently to his mouth, "He is not," she insisted softly.

Henry looked into her pale blue eyes, then searched the rest of her face, a face he had gotten to know better than his own.

She removed her hand, "Do you believe me?"

Henry did not answer. He didn't need to. For it wasn't a matter of believing.

He kissed her, gently at first, then harder, taking her face between his hands. She responded by pressing herself against him, but broke away after a moment.

"It is broad daylight, my lord," she said teasingly, knowing how he enjoyed her calling him that, "People will talk."

He ran a hand down her throat, his thumb tracing the sensitive centre.

"Let them talk," he whispered hoarsely, "If loving one's queen is to be considered a scandal, then may my reign be the most scandalous of all."

91

Chapter 11

It had been a difficult few years for the first Tudor King and Queen. But tragedy did not discriminate, coming for the poor and rich folk alike, never keeping tabs on how much someone had already suffered.

"Dead?"

The word fell – *thump!* – like a boulder between them, and slowly, its meaning impressed on their hearts.

"No," Lizzie mumbled, turning her head in a half shake, her beautiful face contorted in a pained frown, "No, no…"

In a swift motion, Henry took her in his arms and held her to him. She tried to pull away at first, but he held her steady, bearing the brunt of her swift fury at the news.

"*Shh,*" he whispered into her hair, a hand cupping the back of her head as she buried her face in his maroon robe.

They had just retired to their bedchambers, their bedsheets pulled back by the servants, the candles blown out save for the ones by their bedside tables, when the knock at the door had come.

A messenger had entered, his face sombre regardless of the gloom, and the king had immediately known that something was fatally wrong. And yet – to his utter shame – at the messenger's missive, Henry had felt a pinch of relief that it hadn't been about his heir.

"There was nothing we could've done," Henry said now, swallowing the guilt he felt, hoping to comfort his wife, "She's with God, now."

Lizzie, her arms now slack at her sides and her cheek pressed against Henry's firm chest, stared unblinkingly ahead, at the tapestry and the stone wall beneath. Her hand crept up to the growing bump under her nightdress, the babe inside her kicking gently, as if wondering what had happened.

But not even this new child could alleviate Lizzie's pain, and in her mind's eye she saw only her daughter on the day she was born, all pink and wriggly in her arms. Her baby, her namesake… How could she suddenly be gone?

"She'd cried so loudly," Lizzie mumbled then, so low Henry had to ask her to repeat it, "Her cry. She was so strong."

Henry inhaled shakily, then slowly let the breath out, fighting back his sorrow. He had to remain composed. It wouldn't do if they both crumbled.

"Children get sick," he croaked, as if it was just. That. Simple.

"I wish I'd held her a little longer," Lizzie said now, her voice no longer a weak whisper but a full body shudder, "I wish I'd kissed her plump little cheek and listened to her babble…And now…and – now…"

She was weeping suddenly, choking on her own words, on her grief, on her regrets.

Henry held her at arms' length, to look at his wife, "Lizzie, breathe. *Shh*, breathe…"

But she crumpled then, exhausted by the instant heartache that came from the loss of a child. Prepared, Henry caught her in his arms before she fell to the floor and guided her gently down, conscious of her rounded belly.

He sat with her, cross-legged before the unlit hearth, as she continued to hiccough and he continued to coax her to inhale through her nose and out her mouth. He began to worry when Lizzie's hands started to shake, and considered calling for help. But then she took in a great gasp and expelled one long, guttural howl. One that he felt vibrate right through her entire body, until there was nothing left.

The air had turned colder with the change in season, and inside the prince's private chambers, Arthur sat quietly by the fireplace, a book of Latin open before him but unread as he watched the low flames licking lazily at the wood.

He had already read that particular book so often he could almost recite it verbatim. There was really no need to read it again. But his tutor had assigned him a re-read, and though Arthur wasn't actively reading it, he was not brazen enough to blatantly disobey his tutor.

A soft knock at the door broke the prince's solitude, and he quickly straightened his back and pretended to peruse the Latin text, his stomach dropping at the prospect of being caught slacking.

It wasn't his tutor that entered the room, but rather his Chief Gentleman of the Privy Chamber Richard Pole and his wife Maggie.

"Sir Richard," Arthur said in greeting, frowning slightly to see their sombre expressions, "Aunt Maggie, has something happened?"

Though Maggie was Arthur's first cousin once removed, he reserved to calling her aunt, since it mirrored their relationship more closely than cousin, given their age gap.

Maggie and Arthur had grown close since the Pole's transition to the prince's household, Maggie often walking the gardens with him and her three-year-old son Henry, who Arthur was always very patient and gentle with. In recent years, Maggie had developed such a fondness for the young prince that she had even named her newest son after him, baby Arthur.

Maggie looked briefly to her husband, wondering if he would begin, but then quickly thought better of it. On a personal level, she was a lot closer to the prince than her husband was. And the kind of news they were bringing should come from someone who Arthur loved.

"Is it news from my Lord Father?" the prince asked.

Maggie's heart ached, and she hesitated a moment before producing a letter.

"It is, Your Grace. From the king and queen."

Arthur took the letter hesitantly, noting the familiar seal with the Tudor Rose. He broke it open and scanned the written lines. Then he stopped.

"She's…" he looked up at Maggie and Sir Richard, confusion clouding his young face, "She's gone?"

He looked at the letter again, rereading the words as if he might have misunderstood. But he had not.

His fingers tensed, the paper crinkling slightly in his hands.

"She was only three," he said quietly, "I think – I think she had golden hair? Like Mother's?" he looked up at Maggie with tears in his eyes, hoping to find confirmation. Hoping to find that he had remembered his little sister correctly.

Maggie stepped forward, her maternal instinct to protect sparking inside her. But Arthur was not her son, and to reach out to the Prince of Wales would not be appropriate.

"I can't quite remember," Arthur went on quietly, "I haven't seen her in two years…since I left."

Richard Pole swallowed audibly, looking over at his wife.

"We will hold a mass for her," Pole said, trying to alleviate some of the prince's pain in the only way he knew how.

Arthur wiped away the tears, then sniffed and nodded, clasping his hands behind his back. Poised even in heart-wrenching grief. But underneath the rigid stance, Maggie continued to see a hint of something, a tremor of uncertainty, one she was all too familiar with given her own childhood, her own lost sibling. Teddy may not be dead, but Maggie had lost him all the same, for isolation and imprisonment in the Tower for so many years had turned his mind to mush.

Empathy seized the lady's heart, and a saddening notion crossed her mind: for all Arthur's royal training in adult affairs, no one could ever be prepared for the tragedy of losing someone they loved.

<u>December 1495</u>

At a time when Henry VII did not think things could get any worse, they did.

"The physicians called it a 'weakness of the chest'," his mother Margaret Beaufort told him as tears shone in her bloodshot eyes, "They could do little beyond warming cloths and muttering prayers."

"It was his heart then," Henry mumbled, stunned by his uncle's sudden death, surprised that, of all the many ways one could leave this world, it would be Jasper's heart – once as resolute as his sword arm – that would betray him.

"He – He…They say he could no longer stand," Margaret continued, emotion overcoming her, for she and Jasper had been close ever since she'd married his brother at just twelve-years-old. Jasper had been like a brother to her, and like a father to Henry.

"He could no longer climb the stairs –" she blubbered, pressing her hand to her face.

Henry rose from his throne and walked towards his mother, unable to see her hurting, though he was himself struggling to remain composed. He took her in his arms and she sobbed quietly, Henry suddenly realising that she, too, was no longer a young woman. He could feel the frailness of her body as she wept, each sharp bump of her spine.

"He saw kings rise and fall," Henry muttered pensively as he continued to hold his mother, their roles oddly reversed, "banners torn and blood spilled. He crossed seas with nothing but his name. And though the Tudor line had been perilously close to extinction more than once, he lived long enough to see me crowned. That was more than he'd dared to hope during those long years of exile, when he and I were little more than hunted ghosts. He may not have been my father, and he may not have had sons of his own, but his legacy lives on through me, Lady Mother. Jasper Tudor will not be forgotten."

Margaret nodded her head and stepped back, embarrassed suddenly by her reaction.

She sniffed loudly and wiped underneath her eyes, "Forgive me, Henry," she said, "That was inappropriate."

But Henry met her gaze with compassion. He knew that his mother had always harboured some kind of feelings for his uncle. Perhaps not in the romantic sense, but a deep bond had formed between them, nonetheless, forged before Henry was even born.

"It feels strange without him in it now," Margaret admitted sadly, "The world."

Henry nodded but he did not dare to speak, for he was desperately trying not to show any emotion.

As king, he could not afford to show any cracks.

Jasper had taught him that.

<u>March 1496</u>
<u>Sheen Palace, Surrey</u>

There was not much time for grief, for soon enough, Lizzie was once more in confinement in preparation for the birth of her new baby.

"I pray for a girl," Henry told his mother privately when news had come that the queen's labour had begun, "Lizzie has suffered so much over little Elizabeth's loss."

Margaret Beaufort frowned, her forehead wrinkling.

She had aged visibly, Henry noticed, in the last few months since Jasper's death. The sorrow of his loss – as well as baby Elizabeth's – having wreaked havoc on her skin.

But Henry didn't need to look in the mirror to know that he, too, had grown haggard. Life, no matter how glorious or privileged, would eventually take its toll on a person.

"You should be praying for sons, Henry," his mother reminded him gently.

Henry exhaled, leaning forward in his seat and resting his elbows on his knees, "I have two. And there will likely be more in the future. But a girl might heal Lizzie's heart. It may be exactly what she needs right now."

Margaret, who sat beside him on the lounger by the fireplace, put a hand on his shoulder, "Whether this child be a boy or a girl, it cannot replace the one you have lost."

A pain shot through Henry's chest.

Henry and Margaret were not overly affectionate. Lord knew she had always wished they were, but the many years that they had been separated during Henry's youth had created a distance between them. They were mother and son, with common goals and beliefs. But they did not have a natural, familial bond. The time he had held her after Jasper's death had felt both precious and peculiar all at once.

Which is why, when Henry reached up to grasp his mother's hand as he continued to stare pensively at the glowing embers, her heart leapt with delight.

"Elizabeth's loss pains me still," Henry admitted quietly, and Margaret's throat constricted, knowing he would never dare to admit to that aloud to anyone. She felt privileged he did so to her.

"I can only imagine," she replied in a weighted whisper, never having experienced the loss of a child, for she had only ever dared to have one, "If I had lost you, I believe I might have died a little. Inside."

Henry nodded his head and squeezed her fingers before letting go. Margaret's hand felt cold with the absence of his, but she took his queue and withdrew her hold from his shoulder.

A knock at the door made them both turn around then, their eyebrows high on their foreheads in anticipation of the news.

"Your Grace, my Lady the King's Mother," the messenger said, bowing, "I bring happy news! The queen has delivered. She and the child are healthy."

"Such a swift birth!" Margaret beamed, remembering her own long and arduous experience and crossing herself.

The messenger nodded, "It is a girl, Your Highness. A princess!"

Henry stood so quickly from his seat his head swam, "A girl?"

"Yes, Your Grace. She is healthy and is already at the wetnurse's breast."

Margaret smiled tearily at her son, "God answered your prayers."

Henry nodded, though he felt guilty suddenly for thinking his lost daughter could be so easily replaced with another.

The messenger left, and Henry hung back for a moment, watching him go.

"We shall call her Mary," the king said, "And we will cherish her until the end of our days."

He looked down at his mother beside him, "But you are right, Mother. She cannot replace Elizabeth. No child should carry such a burden. And no parent can so easily forget."

June 1496
Ludlow Castle, Shropshire

Griffith Rhys laughed at Arthur's quip and tousled his hair when John Almor's sharp voice rang through the air.

"Hands off the prince," Almor reminded Griffith, irked that he continued to treat Arthur like a child when he was a young man, a future king, "Remember your status, Rhys. Remember the prince's."

Griffith did not need to reply, his exasperation being quite clear on his face.

Arthur, his gloved arm poised to hold steady his falcon, chuckled softly at Griffith's expression, then turned and frowned up at Almor. But his gaze did not linger on him, for behind his head of security there approached two envoys and a man.

Griffith cleared his throat and nodded at the prince's falconer, who stepped forward to take the great brown bird from Arthur. The prince thanked him under his breath, rubbing at his arm as the men stopped before him.

The guards bowed, then turned in unison and left, their mission to deliver the man complete.

"Your Grace," Almor said, standing between him and the man, "This is Bernard André, your new tutor."

"New tutor?" Griffith asked, speaking aloud what Arthur dared not.

André, dressed in a long black habit, a black leather girdle and a white scapular tied with a cord, indicating him to be a friar, bowed at the waist. Arthur's eyebrows twitched, noticing he directed his bow towards Griffith. He was about to correct the man that it was he who was the prince when Almor quickly interjected.

"André is blind, Your Grace, you must forgive him his poor mark."

"My apologies, Your Grace," André said, straightening up and staring unseeingly at the sky with blue-white eyes, "I heard a voice and assumed it was the prince."

"Griffith spoke out of turn," Arthur said, hoping to guide the man to his location with his voice, "But he stated only what I, too, thought. Are you to replace John Rede?"

"Indeed!" André said, smiling joyfully, flashing a row of crooked teeth.

Arthur flinched slightly to think how easy it was for people to leave him behind. He had thought Rede had enjoyed his company, as Arthur had enjoyed his – though Arthur *had* become slightly jaded by the repetitiveness of his lessons.

But he pushed aside his childish thoughts. Rede had been paid for his time. Same way any of his household was, in one way or another. If not in coin, then in title, prestige.

He looked over to the young man beside him. Even Griffith was not by his side for friendship alone.

"As a French Augustinian friar, poet, and historian," the blind friar went on, "I will be teaching you further in Roman and Greek history, but also Latin. Your father the king is keen to introduce Your Grace to the latest Italian and French trends in an effort to connect England to networks of scholars in Italy and France. In that regard you have surpassed Rede's abilities. I have been appointed to take over."

Almor nodded sagely and opened his mouth to speak, but André unknowingly cut him off, adding, "And we must improve your Latin if you are to communicate with your betrothed."

Arthur felt his cheeks flush at the mention of the girl he had been promised to since the age of three. At ten years old, he still did not care for the idea of a wife, and the allusion of her brought a rush of mortification to flood his veins.

"Ah, but the prince's Latin is exceptional," Griffith grinned, sensing some of the tension and nudging Arthur gently with his elbow.

Arthur was glad for his friend in that moment – even if their bond had been arranged.

"I have no doubt!" André replied, bowing his balding head, "And yet, with my input, the prince shall be able to send the *infanta* letters in no time."

Chapter 12

<u>July 1496</u>
<u>Greenwich Palace, London</u>

As well as the domestic success of gaining another healthy child, King Henry VII's reign continued to flourish politically, too.

Though England and Burgundy continued to have somewhat of a strained relationship, earlier in the year they had agreed to sign the *Intercursus Magnus* treaty, which secured favourable trading conditions for English merchants and boosted English economy. In addition to that, England had also joined Pope Alexander VI, the Holy Roman Emperor Maximilian I, Ferdinand de Aragon, Venice, and Milan, in the League of Venice, in an effort to force the French to relinquish their hold of Italy.

Internationally, King Henry VII had made great allies.

And yet there were still those who would continue to oppose him.

"Not only has James IV of Scotland welcomed the pretender into his court with open arms," Henry informed his queen following another increasingly vexing council meeting, "But we've now had word that he has married Lady Catherine Gordon!"

Lizzie's eyes widened, then she dismissed her ladies with a wave of her hand, watching them exit in single file before she replied.

"A noblewoman?"

Henry swallowed, searching his wife's face, "Not only a noblewoman, Lizzie. She is a distant relative of King James IV himself. He must truly believe the pretender to be your brother!"

Lizzie shook her head in disbelief, and Henry watched her intently for any sign of – what? Falsehood? Betrayal?

Could his wife *really* have been in on this elaborate, decades-long plot to overthrow him?

But no. Lizzie couldn't. She wouldn't.

Another thought came to mind. Something Lizzie had once mentioned herself.

"Could your uncle really have set them free?"

Henry had whispered the question, as if to speak it aloud could make it true. But even whispered it sounded like a clap of doom between them, and Lizzie, feeling the shift in the air, locked eyes with her husband.

Henry flinched to see fear in them.

"It is possible..." she said slowly, her voice trembling.

Henry groaned and turned away from her, his hands clenching into fists at his sides.

Lizzie slumped into a chair, defeated, and dropped her head into her hands.

A silence befell the couple as both their minds reeled.

Then the queen voiced a thought she would one day regret giving life to.

"Ought we not also prepare our second son for kingship?"

Henry whirled around, a crease between his brows so deep Lizzie flinched.

"Where has your mind gone?" he said, frankly disturbed by his wife's thought process, "Do you think me incapable of keeping this would-be usurper from us? From Arthur?"

She hung her head, "I understand why you sent him away from us. To be brought up to be a king, yes, but also to be separated from us so that he may have a chance of escape if London is taken. But what if *Arthur* is the one who will be taken from us. What if, instead of coming for you, this...pretender...comes for our boy?"

Henry knelt before her and took her hands in his, "No harm will come to our heir, I promise you that."

She nodded – for what else could she do? – and he wiped at her cheek, where tears had left their shiny trail.

"Besides," Henry said, sobering up and returning to his rational mindset, "Educating Harry as we have Arthur would only breed competition between the boys. And the last thing we want is an in-house rivalry."

Lizzie blinked away her remaining tears, then nodded when Henry's words settled in her mind. Family discord was what had led to the Cousin's War. And hers and Henry's legacy was to have put an end to it. Not to reawaken it by raising two potential kings.

"You are right, Henry. Of course," she said, well aware of her younger son's shortcomings. Though she loved Harry deeply, and spoiled him constantly with gifts and attention, unlike Arthur, Harry was not shrewd or tolerant enough to ever be king.

"Then what shall we do about Scotland?" Lizzie said, returning to the matter at hand, "The pretender's marriage to the Lady Gordon symbolically legitimizes his claim. Even if he is not my brother –"

"He is not your brother," Henry countered automatically, a twinge in his voice.

"But even if he is *not*, this marriage gives the boy credibility in the eyes of others."

Henry nodded and stood, running a hand across his chin, his fingertips tracing over an old scar.

"James of Scots wants to weaken England by supporting this rival claimant," he said, "If he is ready to offer up a noble wife for this false prince, then James will be prepared to go to war."

Lizzie rose and followed her husband to where he now stood by the window, overlooking everything and seeing nothing.

"But we are not weak," she said, and Henry turned around to look at her.

"No, we are not," he said, though he was no longer sure if England was united enough in support of him to take on this boy who had incited so much foreign backing.

"Then," Lizzie said, inhaling deeply, her own uncertainty made plain, "Whatever comes our way, we will keep fighting him off, until we seize him."

"And if it turns out he *is* your brother?" Henry asked, surprising even himself, "Where will you stand then? What will you do?"

Lizzie raised her eyes to Henry's, "Brother or pretender. The boy cannot live."

And Henry visibly relaxed at the lack of hesitation in her answer.

<u>September 1496</u>

As King Henry feared, Scotland's support for the pretender did not stop at offering him a wife, and word quickly spread of an invasion from the north.

A Scottish army led by their king and the false York boy made their way into England across the River Tweed in Northumberland, issuing proclamations calling for English support and urging people to rise up against Henry Tudor and restore the rightful Yorkist King, himself.

Henry, receiving word of the invasion, responded by calling his own men to arms, and he readied himself for yet another battle.

He and his English troops were underway from London to the north, however, when word reached them that God had – yet again – smiled down on the Tudor King.

"They have retreated!" John de Vere exclaimed from atop his warhorse with a triumphant grin, receiving the messenger ahead of his king, "The Scottish army stayed but a few days before returning to Scotland! The pretender was largely mocked or ignored when calling locals to arms. They are calling it a mere border raid, rather than an invasion."

Henry breathed a surprised laugh at that, and his army behind him followed suit, grateful to have evaded a bloody skirmish.

"This is good news," Henry said as he contemplated how this might affect the pretender's support. Surely now that the Scottish King had himself seen how little sway the boy had over the English people, he would lose his backing from Scotland. King James IV would be most regretful to have given the pretender a noble Scottish wife, and a relative of the king, no less.

"Good news, indeed, Your Grace!" de Vere replied, his dark eyes shining with delight.

"Except," Henry said then, lifting his gaze, "He has slipped through our fingers again."

De Vere shook his head, "After this failure, he won't be a threat to us for much longer. I am sure of that, Henry."

Chapter 13

As a perpetual outsider among his kin, Arthur had thought that he knew what loneliness felt like. But at Ludlow, where he was set up with an even larger retinue and further secluded from his family, the young boy finally understood that loneliness came from the absence of love, not the absence of society.

Arthur was never alone, being constantly surrounded by servants, grooms, his council, his tutors…and yet despite their relentless presence, Arthur felt more isolated and empty than ever.

Certainly, he had Griffith and his Aunt Maggie, both of whom he had formed meaningful bonds with. He would even go so far as to call Griffith his good friend. But deep down, Arthur believed it was only a matter of time before they would also disappear from his life. Just as everyone else he'd cared about had.

Growing up, Arthur was constantly told how important he was, how special, how needed. But the older he got, the more he came to realise that *being* special did not equate to *feeling* special.

He was the Prince of Wales, the King of England's prized firstborn, the one who would one day follow in the king's footsteps and become the most powerful man in all the realm. And yet, despite all that, Arthur felt as small and insignificant as an ant. An ant that had been separated from its colony.

With the rising of the sun, Arthur pushed the covers off of himself and swung his legs out of bed, despair washing over him the moment his feet touched the ground. The mere thought of another lengthy morning of reading, learning, improving, followed by an afternoon of listening to the humdrum of his council caused him to wish for a catastrophe. Even if only to raise his heartbeat momentarily.

He never did anything purely for the sake of *fun*.

Arthur's stomach turned with aversion – same way the sheer sight of roast pheasant now did, after having voiced his liking of it the previous year and been served it for supper night after night until he declared he would rather starve than ever be served pheasant again.

Perhaps he ought to take the same approach with his tutors, he thought suddenly as he washed his face in the silver basin by his bed. Tell them that he would rather *die* than memorise another poem, or dissect another political tactic from past kings' reigns.

He exhaled dejectedly, patting his face dry with a scented cloth. Of course that would never do. To cause such a stir would only lead to more chaos. His father would no doubt explode. At the very least he would increase Arthur's security, filling his household with more strangers.

When all Arthur really needed was his father's love and affection – *anyone's* love and affection.

Not for what he represented. But for who he was.

<u>June 1497</u>
<u>Greenwich Palace, London</u>

Despite the people's loyalty to their king against the Yorkist pretender when he attempted to invade with Scotland's help, they were not best pleased with the king's actions to retaliate.

"In order to finance a campaign against Scotland, we must raise taxes," the Archbishop of Canterbury and the king's Lord Chancellor John Morton said, raising his bushy white brows, "That is simple enough to understand!"

"Understanding isn't the people's problem," Richard Foxe replied from across the council table, "They simply do not want to pay taxes!"

"Cornwall already harboured resentment against their tax collector," John de Vere added, to further explain the people's discontent.

But the others did not pay attention. Or they didn't care.

"Then they must be *made* to pay!" Morton called hotly.

"You do know they are calling for your head, Archbishop," de Vere clarified, one eyebrow raised in caution, "Surely I need not remind you."

The old man slumped back in his seat then, almost like a scolded child.

"How many have gathered so far for this cause against me, de Vere?" the king asked finally, when a moment of silence had presented itself.

"Over ten thousand have marched into Devon and they continue south. But their support in Devon has been far less than in Cornwall. I do not expect their numbers to grow by much more. What is extraordinary, however, is that they are not being led by a noble man, but by a mere blacksmith and a lawyer."

Henry waved his hand, "The details of their leaders' backgrounds are of no use to me. An uprising of such a scale is treasonous."

He did not need to elaborate, for they all knew what he had left unsaid. A rebellion of that scale had the potential to overthrow the monarch.

He rose from his throne at the head of the table. There was only one reasonable action to take.

"Divert our army from the borders of Scotland," he ordered, "London needs defending."

17th June 1497

There was general alarm among the citizens of London, for the rebels had gathered on Blackheath in the south-east of the city. What they didn't know, however, was that thousands of rebels had deserted the cause the night before, when they were faced with the reality of their actions.

And what the *rebels* didn't know, was that the king was preparing to attack them two days prior to the agreed upon date.

"They did not come here with the intention of committing treason," John de Vere explained as he and Henry were being fitted in their armour, readying themselves for battle, "They want leniency on the taxation, and an alteration to your advisors."

Henry scoffed, "Regardless," he said, staring out of the open window, "Their presence is a threat. No matter their intention."

De Vere nodded, "We have mustered over twenty-five thousand men in our defence. The rebellion has failed to gather enough support to withhold us."

Henry inhaled deeply and expelled his breath before turning to face his principal military commander.

"Good," he said, showing no interest in the mercy de Vere was carefully hinting at, "With their lack of supporting cavalry, I have faith we shall succeed."

King Henry VII's forces consisted of three battalions, deployed so as to surround the high ground of Blackheath where the rebel army had camped. The rebels were well enough prepared to have positioned archers there, and though caught off guard, they did manage to inflict severe casualties on part of the king's army. And yet, overwhelmingly outnumbered, outmanoeuvred, and surrounded, their fight quickly became a hopeless cause. Many rebels were killed, the mud running red with death, and of their leaders, two were captured on the field, while another sought sanctuary in the Friar's Church nearby before being intercepted on the way.

Following the bloody battle, King Henry toured the battlefield, knighting the most valiant of soldiers, and then returning to the city to reward the mayor for feeding his army.

The leaders were executed ten days later, their sentence calling for hanging, drawing and quartering. But Henry VII showed them mercy at the last minute, ordering for them to be merely hanged for their sins. Their bodies were decapitated and quartered after their deaths, and their heads set on spikes on the London Bridge.

The remaining quarters of their lowly leaders were displayed at various points in Cornwall and Devon, as a reminder to the people of those regions that to rise against their king led to swift and grave retribution.

<u>July 1497</u>

King Henry, now forty years old, was standing by the open window of his chambers, overlooking his city. Dressed in a crimson jacket and hose, and a robe of cloth of gold that reached the floor, he was the very image of a strong and noble king.

But inside, he was beginning to question just how strong he really was.

After twelve years on the throne, Henry had come to realise that he was not well liked. No matter how much he tried to do his best for the realm as a whole, no matter how much he stood for peace and tranquillity, it seemed he could not appease all of England at once. This latest rebellion had proven that to be true.

He sighed heavily as his mind whirled with these thoughts, and watched the people below. Gardeners tended to rose bushes, stable boys mucked out the horses' stalls, courtiers wandered the lawns with gossip on their lips. At a mere glance, his people appeared content.

How tragic that some of them would seek to depose him, and he would never know from simply looking at them.

With the sun shining brightly and a gentle breeze cooling the air, one could almost forget that, not two weeks ago, London – and the monarchy – had been on the edge of being overthrown.

Though the king appeared to have the support of his people when it came to the Yorkist pretender, the recent rebellion had opened his eyes to his subjects' fragile happiness.

Being taxed to fund a war on Scotland would not have gone down well regardless, but it was no different a tactic to what any other ruler had done before him! Why then would they dare to march upon the city and intimidate him?!

He shook his head as he thought.

Surely the people understood that in order to defend them from invasion the crown had to be *strong!* And strength came from a raised royal revenue!

Henry, suddenly irked by the people he had been watching, casually going about their lives as though their king wasn't in turmoil, turned away from the window and took a seat at the table. A servant peeled himself from his spot in the corner and poured Henry a cup of wine as he picked up one of the many documents before him. Henry tried to read it, but his mind continued to drift, and he leaned back in his seat with an aggravated exhale, failing to take anything in.

But then, a thought came to him.

Taxing the common folk was not the only way to fund military expenses…

He raised his gold cup to his thin lips and sipped the sweet wine as he thought back to the event which occurred some years prior in 1492, when he had made a bond agreement with Lord Thomas Grey, a Yorkist sympathiser. Henry had never fully trusted Grey – who had attempted to make peace with Richard III instead of backing Henry in 1485 – and in an effort to secure his loyalty, the king had made Grey sign a bond agreement worth ten thousand monies, backed by guarantors, to ensure his good behaviour and loyalty to the Tudors.

Grey never did break his bond agreement.

But what if Henry shackled more nobles to these agreements? Not only would it further solidify their loyalty to the crown, but if they stepped so much as a toe out of line, the king's coffers would benefit greatly. It may not aid him in gaining favour with the nobles, but Henry had learned through the many struggles presented by his subjects over the years that it didn't matter how well liked a monarch was. Only how able he was to defend himself from guaranteed enemy attacks. And money was the only way to achieve that.

The king sighed contentedly at his conclusion, satisfied with himself for having thought of such a clever plan, and he picked up the document he had previously been unable to concentrate on.

Now that he had found somewhat of a conclusion to that issue, King Henry VII could focus all of his attention on the next matter at hand, a matter which had been pending for several years.

His heir's formal betrothal to the *infanta* of Spain, Catalina de Aragon.

Chapter 14

"Don't fret, Arthur," Griffith said as he clapped the younger boy on his slim shoulder, "You aren't to marry the princess today! Not in the flesh, anyhow. It is but the betrothal ceremony." Though he already knew that was the case, Arthur breathed a sigh of relief, his nose filling with the sickly-sweet scent of incense and roses.

"It is demanding all the same," he admitted, shooting a frown at his friend, "You will never know the pressures I am under." Griffith laughed, in the same deep yet measured way as always.

"In that you are correct, Your Grace. No one but you knows the burden you bear," Griffith turned to his young friend then, "But don't forget that you can lean on those you trust to help lighten the load."

Arthur had no time to reply – nor would he have known how to – for the trumpets sounded suddenly to alert the prince that it was time to commence the ceremony.

The air was thick with summer heat, and as Arthur turned the corner and entered the great hall, the walls themselves seemed to warp, leaning in as the court waited in anticipation.

He tugged at his white velvet jacket and raised his chin, his young face pale but composed. Arthur was only eleven, but he had been trained from birth to bear the weight of adult affairs, and he would not falter now, when it seemed like the whole world was watching.

With his head held high and his blue eyes steady, Arthur made his way through the throng of onlookers, noble men and women dressed in their finest, come to observe the significant moment in history.

At the far end of the hall, richly dressed and solemn-eyed, stood the middle-aged Spanish ambassador Roderigo de Puebla, and behind the ambassador, carried in a silver frame and draped in silk, was a painted portrait of the princess Arthur was promised to.

For now however, since she and Arthur were not yet of marital age, Arthur would be speaking his vows to Puebla, a proxy intended standing in for his true betrothed, the *infanta*. And as he took his place beside the dark-haired ambassador, the Prince of Wales glanced at the portrait.

Staring back at him was a blue-eyed, copper haired young princess. He could tell she was dignified, even in paint, with the same controlled poise and grace that Arthur knew all too well from his own expression, one he had been taught to master from an early age. And though he may not yet be ready for marriage, Arthur could not deny that, upon laying eyes on her, he was intrigued.

He wondered then, as the ceremony began, if she too was nervous.

Though far away in Spain, she would be aware of the ceremony taking place in England that day. Same as Arthur, she would also be preparing for a future she could not yet touch, a future she, too, may not yet be ready for.

Latin prayers echoed through the hall then as the bishop intoned the traditional words of betrothal, each sentence feeling like a hammer sealing another nail in the alliance between England and Spain. And soon enough, it was time for Arthur to speak the words he had been practicing all the previous night in the mirror.

"I, Arthur, Prince of Wales, take thee, Catalina de Aragon, for my lawful wife according to the will of God and of this realm."

"Cornwall is still angry following the rebellion," John de Vere informed Henry as he looked up at the king sitting on his throne in the great hall.

"The displaying of the rebellion's leaders' body parts surely did not help in quelling their dissatisfaction!"
This from the king's own mother, Margaret Beaufort, who had made her opinion perfectly clear when her son had first given the order back in June. But at the time Henry had chosen not to listen to a woman's perspective. And now he would pay the price.

"It was nothing short of a spectacle, having the crows feast on their rotting flesh," she added disdainfully, "What else did you expect from the Cornish people at that barbaric act?"

"Mother," Henry mumbled, warning her to hold her tongue. He would not be scolded before his advisors like some young boy. In displaying the corpses of the Cornish Rebellion's leaders for all to see, Henry had hoped to remind the people of that area of who was in charge. But, not three months later, all it had succeeded in doing was aggravate them into another attempt to overthrow their king. This time, with the spurring on of the one man who would not stop being a thorn in Henry's side – the York pretender.
Margaret turned her face away, but Henry could tell from her fervent fingering of her prayer beads that she continued to be disappointed. If only he had listened to his mother's sage advice.

"The York Prince saw an opportunity to ride the wave of Cornish resentment," de Vere said, returning the king's attention to him.
But he had said the wrong thing.

"HE IS NOT THE YORK PRINCE!" Henry bellowed angrily, slamming his fist against the wooden arm of his throne.

De Vere flinched, "O – of course not, Your Highness," he stammered, "I only meant – I meant the *false* York Prince."

"Do not refer to him as such at all," Henry ordered through gritted teeth, "He is a pretender. The Pretender. The Usurper. The Imposter!"

"Regardless what way he is referred to," Foxe interrupted then, taking a step towards his king and breaking Henry's glare from de Vere, "He has landed at Whitesand Bay in Cornwall with a few hundred men. He has declared himself Richard IV and is gathering local support by exploiting Cornish anger towards the crown."

Henry sighed, rubbing at his temple as he thought.

"This time we *will* capture him," he said to no one in particular, his frustration with this matter having reached its precipice, "The Cornish alone will not be enough support to overthrow me. That is if the locals' anger is indeed as raw as we assume."

He saw his mother shake her head from the corner of his eye, and it only made his ire burn hotter.

He would have to set this right if he was ever to wipe that look from his mother's face.

The pretender attracted around six-thousand supporters and formed a second Cornish Rebellion. But as King Henry VII had predicted, it would not be enough.

"The false boy lacks any real military strength," de Vere said as he rode beside Henry at the head of the king's army, squinting against the low autumn sun, "Without Scotland's support following their failed invasion some months earlier, he has no real backing. And though he claims to be the York Prince, I am told he does not possess any leadership ability."

Henry nodded, glad to be reminded of his opponent's weaknesses. Shortly thereafter, as the king and his force continued their march west, another messenger was seen approaching.

"The boy besieged Exeter," the young man panted atop his horse, "in the hopes that it would surrender. But it did not.

Henry grinned, "Excellent. And we are already underway. He will not escape me this time!"

As soon as Henry's troops approached, the pretender's famed bravado was dispersed like dust in the wind, and he abandoned his army to seek sanctuary at Beaulieu Abbey nearby.

Henry and his men chased him down, and had to do little more than wait him out.

It didn't take long for the pretender to surrender, exiting the abbey with his head held high.

But when he emerged, it gave Henry and his men pause.

Before them stood a strapping young man with blonde hair and blue eyes. His body was chiselled with the easy muscles of youth, and upon meeting Henry VII's eyes, a look of determination so vivid crossed his face it made the surrounding soldiers question their resolve.

Quickly enough, however, they came to their senses and seized the man they had been told was an imposter; for if their king was certain of his falsehood, then who were they to doubt it?

With the pretender finally captured, the remaining ringleaders of the rebellion were executed or fined – depending on their involvement. The remaining rebels, of which there were not many, dispersed back to their lives, leaving the pretender to be taken to London to be paraded through the streets on horseback.

There, the prisoner was met with much hooting and derision from the citizens, many having gathered to hurl vegetables, stones, and insults at him as he was taken to the Tower.

But throughout the onslaught of abuse, the young man held his head high, never once showing remorse or fear.

And though he was the one who was bound and guarded, it was Henry VII who felt suddenly ill at ease.

"Is it him?"

Henry asked Lizzie as soon as he entered her chamber later that night, and she could tell from the wild look in his eyes that he had been aching to ask the question all day.

Her ladies bobbed a curtsy and quit the room, leaving the royal couple alone with their fears.

Lizzie blinked, "I don't – I didn't see him well enough. He could – he could be…"

Henry rasped a frustrated groan and raked his slender fingers through his shoulder-length hair.

It needed cutting. That was all Lizzie could think of as she stared at her husband. For she could not bring herself to recall the young man's face. The look of certainty in his eyes…

"You must not visit him," Henry said now, "Do not go to the Tower. You need not be quizzical. We don't need to know if he is truly your brother or not. Because regardless of that fact, he cannot be allowed out."

"But – don't we wish for this nightmare to end? If I can meet him, face to face and ensure that he is not –"

"No!" Henry argued, "To acknowledge him at all would risk our own royal position and the inheritance of our heirs."

Lizzie's heart pinched. She understood the severity of her curiosity all too well. And yet the question as to her Uncle Richard's true actions continued to haunt her.

Had he killed her brothers in the Tower, all those years ago? Had he aided them in their escape? Had someone else?

But no, she had long ago given up her loyalty to her previous life. The opposing houses of York and Lancaster no longer mattered, only their merged house of Tudor.

So then, why was it suddenly so tempting to finally uncover the truth?

"The usurper's name is Perkin Warbeck," Richard Pole informed the prince when news of his arrest had reached Ludlow, "We finally know the pretender's true name and origin. As the king thought, he is but a common boy, the son of a comptroller from Tournai."
Arthur nodded his auburn head, pleased with the news from court. After years of hearing snippets about the pretender's consistent attempts to claim the throne, it was a relief to hear it had finally come to an end.

"The Treaty of Ayton between Scotland and England has also been signed," Pole continued, looking down at the letter in his hands, "Following the failed Cornish Rebellion and Warbeck's capture, Scotland has washed their hands of him, no doubt realising his uselessness. There will be no retaliation of war from us."

"Good," Arthur replied with a sigh, "The Scots have seen to reason. As has my father. Peace should always prevail. Supporting the usurper was a futile attempt on the Scots' part. But I am glad there will be no more strife between our two nations."
Pole bowed and retreated, allowing Arthur to continue his Latin studies.
Since his formal betrothal to his Spanish bride the previous month, where he had first glimpsed her and come to terms with the reality of his situation, Arthur had developed a keen interest in perfecting his Latin, for until she learned English, Latin was the only language the couple had in common.
Though still only eleven years old, Arthur had experienced a growth spurt in recent months, and according to the ambassador of Milan he had even grown taller than other boys his age. Arthur's features had also begun to develop, his once boyish facets having begun to mould and shape into sharper angles,

similar to those of his father. His eyes, though hooded like that of his grandmother Margaret Beaufort, now held a hint of confidence in them, astute and observant where they had once been uncertain and shy. He had a striking grace in his movements, and his tutors often relayed to their king that Prince Arthur was growing into his role with much promise.

"We shall take the horses out later, Griffith," Arthur said after a moment of quiet reading, "Some fresh air will do us good."

Griffith, who sat in the corner with his feet propped up on a table while the prince studied, nodded absentmindedly, engrossed in his own preferred reading material, the Greek mythology poem Ovid's Metamorphosis.

Later, when the young men had had enough of books, they mounted their horses and set off at a gentle trot in the open field within the outer walls of Ludlow Castle.

"Are you looking forward to seeing your family during the Christmastide?" Griffith asked after a while, when their comfortable silence had stretched on long enough.

Arthur nodded once, a smile tugging at the corners of his lips, "I am," he admitted, "It has been too long since I saw Margaret and Henry."

A memory of baby Elizabeth flashed in his mind's eye, poisoning his excitement momentarily. But he discarded the thought. Sometimes, children died. Though tragic, it was the nature of things.

"I look forward to seeing how Harry is doing with his teachings," Arthur voiced, something he had been quietly wondering for some time, "Though he is not learning to rule like I am, I am intrigued to pick his brain."

"In what regard?" Griffith asked, keeping his brown courser in rhythm with Arthur's white one – his pony having long been replaced with a more suitable steed.

Arthur shrugged, "He is six now! It is the age a boy becomes a man. My Lady the King's Mother, our grandmother, will have taught him things – ideas – that I may not have been posed. As a spare, his mind is being shaped differently. I am curious how."

Griffith nodded slowly, though he failed to comprehend the eagerness that accompanied Arthur's statement.

At nineteen, Griffith cared little for such differing perspectives and intrigues into another's mind. As a young man in the throes of adulthood, he was far more interested in the simpler pleasures. But then again, Griffith had not been raised from birth to think like a king, nor to consider what might go on in someone else's head. And he was reminded, once again, how restricted the young prince's life truly was. Never having experienced any delight outside of the curriculum of kingship.

One day, Griffith would have to introduce the young man to life's other enjoyments. Enjoyments beyond that of analysis and learning.

December 1497
Sheen Palace, London

The great hall of Sheen Palace was alight with shimmering candlelight and blazing hearths, the scent of orange and clover thick in the air. Long tables groaned under the weight of dozens of silver plates, filled with roasted meats, gilded marchpane figures, and spiced wine.

Seated at the high table beside his royal father, Prince Arthur sat straight-backed and serious – mimicking the king – as he observed the merry court.

Prince Harry sat on Arthur's other side, and in complete contrast to his older brother, Harry was already full of laughter and mischief, having spent his childhood being just that – a child.

"Stop it, Harry," Arthur mumbled quietly for what felt like the tenth time, as his young brother continued to swing his legs beneath the table, his velvet shoes occasionally kicking Arthur in the shins.

Harry, ignoring his older brother's request, leaned closer.

"Arthur," he whispered, the gap in his teeth causing him to lisp, "Want to go play?"

Arthur glanced at the freckly boy from the corner of his eyes without turning his head, as if afraid to be seen speaking out of turn, "The feast has not yet concluded."

Harry frowned briefly, then grinned, "Says who?"

"Says the king."

The young prince *humphed* then, crossing his arms over his chest, "No one will be made to suffer this boredom when I am king."

Arthur couldn't help but smile at his brother's tone – so petulant, something he had never been allowed to be – and he was equal parts disturbed and amused by his words.

Further down the table, their mother the queen peered across her husband and offered her sons a soft smile. It warmed Arthur's heart. Though, deep down, he knew the smile grew wider only for the sight of Harry.

Arthur had never been told as much, but the painful thought had often crept into his subconscious: that their mother had a favourite between them. And that it wasn't her firstborn.

Just then, a troupe of jesters tumbled into the hall shouting 'Hey! Hey!' and jingling their caps, interrupting Arthur's wallowing. A falconer followed, carrying a hooded bird perched on his glove. Arthur leaned forward slightly, eyes narrowing with focus.

"That's a gyrfalcon," he murmured.

But Harry beside him was too busy giggling at the jester balancing a pie on his head to pay attention to his brother.

Later, after the feasting and entertainment, the princes were led to the hearth where a Yule log crackled with flames.

"Care for a game of chess?" Arthur asked, gesturing towards the table. Arthur was curious as to Harry's skill. At six, Arthur could already beat his then tutor at the game. Would Harry be as proficient as he?

Harry climbed up onto his seat, claiming the white pieces, "My white knights are braver than yours!"

"I doubt it," Arthur replied, somewhat smugly, as he slid into his chair.

"They are! I'll show you!"

Before it could turn into a tussle, Margaret Beaufort swept towards them, moving with purpose even in her heavy robes.

Arthur's back immediately straightened at her presence, while Harry remained slack and indifferent.

Arthur envied him his nonchalance. His ability to be at ease.

"Princes of England do not squabble over victory," she said, though not unkindly, "You are brothers. Remember that always."

"Yes, Lady Grandmother," they chorused, before readying their game, the musicians' song wafting quietly through the air from the far corner.

Arthur defeated Harry with but six moves the first time, causing the younger boy to gawk confusedly before resetting the pieces. It crossed Arthur's mind, as they began their second game, that Harry was most likely not used to winning because he was any good, but rather because he was allowed to win.

But Arthur wouldn't go easy on him. Everything else was just handed to his younger brother, and he would not disrespect him like that. Harry had a good head on his shoulders, Arthur could tell. He just needed to be made to use it.

But before their second game could gain momentum, Harry gasped and craned his neck.

"Look!" he said enthusiastically, grinning mischievously, "It's Warbeck."

Arthur turned his attention to where most of the court were suddenly looking and was surprised to see a good-looking young man who – despite being made to wear servant's attire – exuded confidence.

"What is he doing here?" Arthur asked, to which Harry scoffed a laugh, reminding Arthur of how out of touch he was with the court, how he was a stranger within his own family.

"As soon as he confessed to being a fraud," Harry's young boy voice explained, "he was released from the Tower and given accommodations at Father's court."

Arthur's eyebrows shot up in surprise, and Harry leaned forward over the chess table, knocking over his bishop – though he seemed no longer to care – and whispered conspiratorially.

"He is kept under guard, of course," he lisped, "But as you can see, he is allowed to be present at royal banquets, though he is returned to his lowborn status."

"Father is certainly forgiving," Arthur voiced, wondering briefly how he would have dealt with the situation if he were king. Would he have been as magnanimous as his predecessor? Or would he have acted first in dispatching the pretender before he could attempt an escape or another coup?

"Ha!" Harry barked, snickering from behind his hand, a hand Arthur noticed was still so small, "The king has not allowed him to live because he is forgiving."

Arthur frowned briefly, but understanding quickly followed.

He looked back at the young man, who was refilling lords and ladies' wine cups.

"No, of course not," Arthur said, "Our father wishes to belittle him. To show the world Warbeck is not a threat by parading him as a mere servant, someone of little worth. Certainly not someone the king would worry about."

Harry nodded once, then yawned, suddenly bored of the conversation, though Arthur's interest had only just piqued.

"Precisely," Harry said, before hopping off his seat and throwing a quick look at Arthur over his shoulder, "I'll beat you next time, brother!" he said, then ran off into the crowd.

Arthur looked down at the unfinished chess game before him – his rook only one move away from claiming Harry's king, an indisputable Checkmate – and he chuckled quietly to himself as he tidied the pieces away.

Arthur may not always be the first in the know about court dramas, but when it came to strategy and discipline, his little brother still had a lot to learn.

Prince Arthur lay on the left side of the four-poster bed, his hands tucked underneath his cheek as he smiled in his sleep in response to a dream. He was hawking in his dream, his arm perched and gloved, his eyes fixed on his favourite falcon as it flew high in the air, its beautiful brown wings a sharp contrast to the vibrant blue of the sky.

The scent of spiced wine and orange was still thick in the air from the night's festivities, and as Arthur sighed contentedly in his sleep, a waft of it infiltrated his subconscious, steering him to dream instead of the many delicious dishes from the night before: marchpane, roast peacock and spiced fruits. In his vision, he plucked a sugared grape from before him and popped it in his mouth, the sound of joy and laughter echoing all around him. Though no one in the crowd had a face.

Suddenly, his dream transformed in his mind's eye, causing him to flinch slightly, but not enough to rouse him. Gone were the silver plates of food, the sweet taste in his mouth replaced with that of ash, the faceless courtiers and their laughter dispersed like smoke.

Smoke.

Too much smoke.

And then…mayhem.

"Wake up, Your Grace!"

His guard was calling above all the other noise: shrill screaming, bells tolling, heavy footsteps, doors slamming.

"Fire!"

Arthur practically fell out of bed, smacking his knee on the wood floor and inhaling sharply through gritted teeth. The guard slung his arm around Arthur's waist and heaved him upright, then grabbed him forcefully by the arm and pushed him forward.

"Down the staircase and through the courtyard!" the guard shouted, falling behind for a moment as a wood beam collapsed between them.

Arthur stopped, purely out of shock, and looked back at the guard, wide-eyed. He motioned with wild gestures for Arthur to keep going, but the prince only did so when he was certain the guard could get around the burning beam.

Others were rushing out of their chambers, his mother's ladies, Lady Darcy, his sister Margaret.

"This way!" Arthur called to them, taking off running again only after he was sure Margaret had seen him.

Coughing and spluttering, Arthur stumbled out into the courtyard, the cold night air feeling like a blessing on his skin.

A panicked exclamation engulfed him, many voices chorusing the same relieved cry to see the heir to the throne come out of the burning palace.

He was suddenly in someone's arms, and through the bitter tang of smoke he could smell the unique scent of his mother.

"Arthur," she croaked, whether from the fumes or emotion, he could not know.

He continued to hold onto his mother but turned in her embrace, desperate to make sure everyone he cared about had made it out safely.

"Where is Harry?" he asked, panic gripping his heart.

"Here," a little voice meowled, and Harry peeked out from behind their mother's skirts.

"Everyone is safe," his father said then, stepping into his line of sight.

His mother let go of him then, almost as though to embrace him was inappropriate, a sign of weakness in the king's presence.

Arthur sniffed, the fire, the smoke and the panic making his eyes and nose run.

"What happened?" he asked, turning to watch the flames as they consumed Sheen Palace, guards, servants, stable boys, grooms, all calling frantically and rushing to and from the river with buckets, trying to douse the fire.

No one gave an answer, and Arthur wondered if that meant they did not know, or that they *did*.

"Let it burn," the king said after a moment, so quietly it may have been to himself, "It will be rebuilt stronger."

And Arthur couldn't help but think, *Had someone in their court just tried to kill the entire royal family?*

Chapter 15

<u>May 1498</u>
<u>Richmond Palace, London</u>

The fire at Sheen Palace had lasted three hours and had torn through a large part of the fortress, causing hundreds to flee in panic.

Thankfully, there were no casualties.

Henry VII did not allow the disaster to vex him, however, deciding instead to use the opportunity presented to rebuild the palace to his own liking.

Construction began, Henry renaming his creation Richmond Palace in honour of the title he had held before ascending to the throne – Earl of Richmond – which he had inherited from his father.

To avoid repeated disaster, Henry had the palace rebuilt largely using brick and white stone, rather than the wood floors and beams it had been made of before. Though it retained the layout of Sheen Palace, Henry ordered new additions, including long galleries to display sculptures and portraiture. He also established a library and a richly appointed chapel. Instead of the slit-like windows of a castle, Henry also ordered for panelled windows to be installed, to bring more light into his new and improved palace.

Following its transformation, Richmond Palace quickly became King Henry's favourite residence, which he made especially clear by the amount of time he and his court would go on to spend there.

The source of the fire had been identified shortly after the flames had been contained, though the king never did share his men's findings with anyone but his queen, for fear of appearing foolish.

But gossip was not an easy beast to tame, especially one as salacious as that, and soon enough the whole English court knew that it had likely been caused by the king's own recklessness.

An unattended candle said one courtier, according to Henry's spies.

A rogue ember, said another.

But worst of all: a divine warning.

Henry did not believe that to be true. After all, God had always been on his side, ever since his victory at Bosworth Field. Granted he had thrown some obstacles his way in the form of Lambert Simnel and Perkin Warbeck, as well as some disputes with France and Scotland. But it was nothing he had not handled with confidence. Each problem finding a solution in his favour.

No, God was not done with him just yet. Of that, he was sure. And soon enough the rumours died down in favour of another scandal, there never being a shortage of them in the English court.

June 1498
Ludlow Castle, Shropshire

"He tried to escape?" Arthur asked over supper eight months later, sure he'd misheard.

Griffith made a noise of affirmation as he reached across the table and ripped a leg off the roast chicken at its centre.

"Didn't make it far, though," he said, "He fled to Syon Monastery but was quickly recaptured."

Arthur shook his head in disbelief at the pretender's audacity.

"My father was allowing him to live freely at court," he protested, "And now he has thrown it away."

Griffith sucked grease off his thumb and forefinger, his eyes narrowing slightly at Arthur's remark.

"You do know he wasn't free," he said tentatively, gently coaxing the younger boy to understand the many dynamics of this situation.

Arthur tutted, "Yes, technically he was not free. But the king allowed him to live despite his repetitive acts of treason."

As he spoke, Arthur could hear the voice in his mind that reminded him it wasn't kindness which led his father to keep Warbeck alive, but a savvy political tactic. The king did not care for the young man's wellbeing. He was not being a noble sovereign. He was being a cunning one.

"Well, he won't get away with it this time," Griffith continued with a shrug, "Perkin Warbeck has been put back in the Tower, alongside the Earl of Warwick, I hear."

"Teddy?" Arthur said, having heard stories of his Aunt Maggie's low-witted brother.

Griffith nodded, "I hear he cannot tell the difference between a goose and a capon."

His friend's soft laughter flared something up in Arthur then, some instinctive need to defend his distant cousin though he had never met him and likely never would.

"He has been imprisoned since the age of ten," Arthur reminded Griffith, a hint of ire in his tone, "I doubt he has had the opportunity for education, much less the possibility of *seeing* geese and capons in his prison cell to learn to distinguish them." Griffith shrugged again, unaware of Arthur's displeasure.

"All the same," he went on between mouthfuls of chicken, "The Perkin Warbeck pretender is locked up. Your father will finally be able to rest easy knowing no one is plotting to overthrow him any longer."

Arthur nodded absentmindedly at that, his thoughts still on Teddy, and how, despite the obvious differences to their circumstances – Arthur's titles, prospects, and relative liberty – the two boys' fates were perturbingly parallel.

For they were both held captive at the king's will, isolated from the outside world and shaped into their respective moulds in order to secure Henry VII's legacy.

September 1498
Greenwich Palace, London

Preparations for Arthur's marriage to Catalina de Aragon had been underway for almost the entire lives of the two royal children.
But more recently, King Henry had started to feel a change in the air.
"Things have changed since we first signed the Treaty of Medina del Campo all those years ago," Henry was telling his advisors following the arrival of another letter from Spain, "And I can tell from these correspondences that they are losing interest."
He threw the letter across the table and sighed, running his hand over his aging face.
"The steadiness I promised England with my ascension has been mocked constantly! First by Lambert Simnel and now by Warbeck!"
"But the two offenders are both under lock and key, Your Highness," Richard Foxe said, looking around at the other advisors, who nodded in conformity, "Their threat has been quashed."
"And yet, Spain is hesitant to conclude this alliance!"
De Vere reached over and picked up the discarded letter from the middle of the table. He had read it already, but in an effort to quell the king's fears, he perused it once more.
"They speak of English chaos," Henry said, voicing aloud what his advisor was reading, "They fear my dynasty is not secure enough to ensure their daughter's future as Princess of Wales. They do not share our enthusiasm for Warbeck's capture."

De Vere looked up from the letter, "Forgive me, Your Highness, but it seems to me they are more concerned with the Earl of Warwick."

Henry frowned.

"See here," de Vere said, pointing to a sentence, "'Yorkist blood'."

"It does not matter," Foxe interrupted frustratedly, "If Spain breaks our alliance before it has formed, England will be weak. We cannot let this treaty go to waste! We have worked over a decade to obtain it!"

"Foxe is right," another councilman added, "Whatever they wish from us, we ought to consider giving it to them."

"They fear Teddy Plantagenet more than Perkin Warbeck," Henry VII said later that day as he stared pensively at the fire in the hearth, the queen and his mother standing behind him.

"Teddy has been placid and imprisoned without issue for over a decade!" Lizzie protested, immediately disturbed by the strange shift in demeanour from Spain.

She rested a hand over her rounded belly, the babe within kicking her as though he could sense her distress.

"Despite that," Henry replied, turning to her, "King Ferdinand and Queen Isabella fear those with York blood. They do not wish to send their daughter to us if there is any possibility of York insurrection."

Lizzie blinked, dumbfounded, at her husband, "There is nothing we can do about that," she said, a statement, but also a plea, "Tell them Teddy is safely locked away. He has been imprisoned, his life wasted in order to secure our reign. Tell them he is no threat!"

She noticed a quick look being exchanged between her husband and her mother-in-law, and she turned her attention to Margaret.

"You know my cousin is no threat to us," Lizzie repeated, her pale cheeks flushed with increasing worry.

Margaret opened her mouth to speak but Henry's voice called her attention back to him, "He is no threat," he agreed, "But we must consider what we ought to do if we wish for our heir to conclude this advantageous marriage. The marriage we have been working on for a decade!"

Lizzie rounded on Henry, her usually soft expression twisted with hurt, "I promised Maggie that Teddy would not be harmed. No, in fact, I promised her I would speak for him, all those years ago, when he was first imprisoned. I never did. For fear for myself, for my sisters, for the children we went on to have. I failed my cousin. And then the Simnel Rebellion sealed Teddy's fate. I have learned to live with my guilt for not speaking up sooner, I have pushed it aside in my mind, even telling myself that his imprisonment had saved his life during the rebellion, for he would surely have been cut down in battle. But I cannot refrain from speaking up now. Henry, he is a child. Perhaps no longer in years but certainly in mind. What treason has he ever committed besides being born?"

Margaret cleared her throat then, moved by Lizzie's words, though a little disturbed by her tone when addressing the king.

"You must not get too upset," she said, "Think of the child in your womb."

Lizzie sighed in frustration, her eyes remaining fixed onto Henry, "Please, Your Highness," she beseeched.

But it was the king's mother who replied again.

"Teddy Plantagenet will remain where he is," Margaret assured her, "We will continue correspondence with Spain and come up with an agreement. They will see to reason, I am sure."

The soft padding of fading footsteps told Lizzie that her mother-in-law had retired from the conversation, and though she took some comfort from Margaret's reply, Lizzie could not bring herself to look away from Henry. After all, *he* was the king. No matter how much power Margaret held, it was his word that would be final.

"Do you concur with your mother?" she asked, bristling a little at her own brazenness. Never had she dared to confront her husband in such a manner, and so blatantly.

Henry stared back at her, worrying on his bottom lip as he thought. But there was nothing he could say in rebuttal to his mother's response, for Teddy was an innocent, unblemished from treacherous intent. And to order his death or even his exile from England without cause would only come back to haunt him.

"Teddy is innocent," Henry finally said.

But his stomach immediately dropped with guilt to see Lizzie's shoulders sag with relief. Because, in the very moment that he had spoken the words aloud, a thought cropped into his mind like an unwelcome weed.

What if...he was not.

<u>May 1499</u>

Prince Arthur's palms were sweaty with nerves; he was not ready to be someone's husband.

At thirteen years old, how could anyone be ready for such a task? He had been fast tracked through childhood, yes, but marriage meant a lifelong commitment, marriage meant unlocking adult concepts Arthur wished not even to consider.

He was not like Griffith, who often spoke about which lady he thought was pretty, or which maid he had flirted with, or which servant girl he had had, with as much gusto as he would discuss a successful hunt. Arthur did not care for the details – though Griffith shared them anyway. He would much rather have discussed the weather.

It was not that girls did not interest Arthur, of course they did. He was a boy on the verge of manhood, with two perfectly good eyes which could appreciate a beautiful lady when he saw one. But he did not have the same easy confidence Griffith had when speaking to women. He could never imagine simply striding up to a particular one and striking up a flirtatious conversation, much less dare to *touch* one!

Which was why, when Arthur was told that he would be marrying the Spanish Princess, he had very nearly failed to remain upright.

"It is a proxy wedding," Richard Pole went on to explain, and Arthur breathed a long sigh of relief.

"A proxy wedding," the young prince repeated, his shoulders relaxing.

"Yes, Your Grace," Pole replied, "to further strengthen our countries' promised alliance. It is but another formal ceremony, much like your official betrothal. Ambassador Don Gutierre Gómez de Fuensalida will stand in for the *infanta*."

Arthur nodded, though his logical mind was already whirring as to why yet another ceremony for this union was necessary, when they had been promised to one another since the ages of three and were already formally betrothed only two years prior.

"Has the Pope failed to grant dispensation?" Arthur asked, furrowing his brow as he considered what may be standing in the way which would make his father feel like further securing Arthur's marriage.

Pole nodded his head at the question, "No, Your Grace. He granted it back in 1497. All is in order. You mustn't worry."

But Arthur wasn't worried, he was curious.

Had something happened for his mother and father to so desperately need to fortify Spain's vow to England?

<u>19th May 1499</u>
<u>Bewdley, Worcestershire</u>

Despite Arthur's hidden hesitation to the idea of marriage, his bride, and adult affairs, he was able to disguise his insecurity. At least while the *infanta* was still thousands of miles away and across the sea.

"I rejoice to contract the marriage," he told his Aunt Maggie on the morning of his proxy wedding, the words sounding rehearsed even to him, "for my love for the princess is deep and sincere."

Maggie had smiled at Arthur affectionately, charmed by his words but not fooled by them.

She knew all too well what it felt like to be made to marry someone you did not know at much too young an age. And she believed it must be harder still for Arthur who had had this union looming over him since before he could properly walk or talk.

She watched him straighten his gold stitched jacket then, before walking confidently towards the Spanish Ambassador at the makeshift altar.

She felt for the poor boy, born into greatness but never to experience the simple joys of life.

Though Maggie hadn't been around during Arthur's early childhood, she had seen enough over the last few years in his household to know that Arthur had missed out on the most basic of human experiences.

She had tried to rectify this terrible mistake by sneaking him out into the courtyard at night, sometimes to watch the stars in the sky, sometimes to talk about frivolities. She had beamed with delight when she had made him laugh at a joke one time, realising in that moment that she had never heard him truly belly-laugh like that before. And the realisation quickly dampened her joy.

No child should grow up the way Arthur had done. Hidden away, secluded from loved ones, denied of his innocence.

It made her think of her brother Teddy.

To Maggie, he and Arthur held many similarities. Which was perhaps why she felt so heartbroken to witness Arthur's silent melancholy, the same way her brother had been in the early years of Henry Tudor's reign, when Maggie had still had the strength to visit him.

But she hadn't seen her brother in years now, not since she had visited him after having her first son, Henry.

She could still recall the weight of the guilt that had pressed upon her heart to tell him of how her life had developed outside of the Tower walls. In those days, she had always come with news from court, of the developments in King Henry's reign, and in her own life. But speaking the sweet words that Teddy had become an uncle had somehow tasted sour upon voicing them aloud. For what good was that news to him, her imprisoned brother, when he would never watch the child grow up. Same way he had never been given the chance to grow up himself.

Maggie knew he was not dim-witted, as many people claimed. Teddy Plantagenet had been astute, kind and bold in his youth. Maggie remembered that clearly. But his many years of imprisonment had warped his mind, stunted it, so that, while his body continued to change into that of a man, his intellect remained that of a child.

Unlike Teddy, Maggie thought presently as she watched Arthur from within the crowd as he recited the bishop's words, Arthur would at least get to lead his own life one day. A life that was not restricted or controlled by others.

He may not have had the chance to run and play and laugh in his youth as other children had, but Arthur Tudor's whole life was still ahead of him. And Maggie had no doubt that he would make the most of it when the time came for him to truly live it.

For the sake of Teddy's unsolicited sacrifice, Maggie prayed that that would be true.

Chapter 16

<u>20th November 1499</u>
<u>Ludlow Castle, Shropshire</u>

"No, no, no, he couldn't! Teddy would never, he *couldn't!*"
Maggie Pole half slumped, half fainted into her husband's steady arms when news of her brother's supposed treason reached her at Shropshire.

"There must be some explanation," Richard said calmly, gently guiding her down onto the lounger at the foot of their bed, "He has not been at risk of flight for the fourteen years he's been imprisoned."
Maggie flinched at the reminder of how long it had been since Teddy had tasted freedom, and the knot of guilt she'd grown to live with tightened in her stomach.

"I feel sick," she mumbled, her mouth filling with saliva, ready to expel their evening meal.
Richard rushed to the door and ordered for a bucket to be brought up, but Maggie managed to contain it, breathing steadily until the hot flush of her ears subsided.

"There must be some mistake," she whispered, looking up at Richard as he sat down beside her and took her hand in his, anchoring her, "Teddy is innocent. He has *always* been innocent."
Richard was nodding, "Perkin Warbeck must be behind this. No doubt some plot gone awry and he has managed to drag your brother into it. Teddy cannot be punished for another man's actions."
Maggie appreciated the way Richard defended her brother so easily, though they knew not of the facts.

"Do you really think so?" she asked, her voice cracking, and feeling suddenly more vulnerable and scared than ever before.

Richard blinked pensively at her before answering.

"Of course."

And though Maggie wanted to believe him – this stranger-become-husband who had been a blessed comfort to her for years – in that one second of doubt, Maggie saw the truth. Even though he had tried to shield her from it.

<u>28th November 1499</u>
<u>The Tower of London</u>

Teddy awoke that morning to the sound of jangling keys and a loud *clunk* as the lock on his cell door was opened.

With a yawn, the young man stretched his arms above his head and smacked his lips, the same way he did every morning at the prospect of breakfast.

But it wasn't a plate of bread or a bowl of gruel that Teddy spied in the guard's hands, but a pair of solid metal shackles.

Teddy looked from them up into the guard's face, frowning when he did not recognise him.

"Am I to be released?" he said, his voice still groggy from sleep.

The guard's jaw twitched with an emotion Teddy couldn't quite place. Confusion maybe? Or uncertainty?

Teddy smiled at the man, trying to put him at ease.

"Come with me," the guard said then, stepping forward to snap the shackles into place around Teddy's wrists.

Teddy obliged, raising his hands before him.

"Am I to breakfast outside?" he asked, turning his head to look out the window, expecting a glorious beam of sunlight.

But the sky was a dark grey, with a light spatter of rain falling at an angle.

Teddy frowned, realising suddenly that something sinister was afoot. His stomach dropped as he turned back around, and the guard grabbed the chain between his wrists and pulled him gently behind him.

"Have I done something wrong?" the young man asked, sounding not like the twenty-four-year-old man he was, but like the ten-year-old boy he had been when he had first been imprisoned in the Tower.

The guard did not respond, which only increased Teddy's nervousness.

His shackles began to chime then, a pretty tune, albeit completely out of place. Teddy looked down at them and realised it was he who was creating the sounds, the shaking of his hands causing the metal restraints to clatter.

"Has my sister come to see me?" Teddy asked, one last ditch attempt at finding out what was going on, "Is Maggie here?"

The guard only shook his head, continuing down the stone staircase with Teddy close behind, their footsteps echoing eerily around them.

When they reached the bottom of the stairs, the guard led him out the door and towards the outer gate. But Teddy did not register his surroundings, for despite the glum weather, he squinted clumsily against the morning glare. His eyes were no longer used to such pure light of day.

At the outer gate, Teddy was handed over to two other men, who the guard greeted with a nod before turning around and heading back.

Teddy watched him go for a moment, then faced the two new men before him. Maybe they would know where he was going? But they, just like the guard, ignored him, taking Teddy roughly by the arm and pushing him forward.

Teddy didn't have to walk for long before he saw it, however, the answer to all his questions. And yet he could not stop asking them, his mind and mouth running wild at the terrifying sight of the scaffold.

"Am I free?"

"Have I done something wrong?"

It never occurred to Teddy, as he was led up the stairs and pushed down onto his knees before the axeman, that every one of his questions would have been answered with a simple 'no' had they only granted him that respect.

But they had not wanted to terrify the young man in his final moments.

Especially given that it would only have been to his final query that Teddy might have gained some peace had they answered.

<u>December 1499</u>
<u>Richmond Palace, London</u>

"There was no other way," King Henry said, repeating the words for what felt like the hundredth time, "Ferdinand de Aragon would never have sent his daughter to marry Arthur if there was even a *remote* possibility of a York uprising!"

Lizzie did not respond, continuing simply to stare out the window, one delicate hand raised to her mouth, her fingers tracing her top lip.

She was deep in thought, Henry knew, but he needed her to answer.

Lizzie hadn't spoken to him since Perkin Warbeck's execution on the 23rd of November. Not because she believed Warbeck to have been her brother, but because she knew that his execution would undoubtedly have led to her cousin Teddy's.

And she had not been wrong.

"The future of England was at stake," Henry continued, trying to convince her that what he had ordered had been for the greater good, "Arthur's future! Teddy was collateral damage. He tried to *escape!* It was treason!"

He was rambling, not even truly believing some of what he said.

Lizzie turned her head to look at him, her blue eyes glassy, like melting ice.

In her expression he could read a dozen responses: *There are plenty of other princesses. Executing Warbeck alone would have been enough.*

But it was the final flicker in her eyes that struck him, causing him to catch his breath. A flicker that said: *Who are you?*

"I did it for us…" Henry mumbled finally, dropping his arms at his sides, defeated.

And that was when Lizzie finally broke the silence between them, after over a week of endless, unspoken torture.

She sighed, a deep exhale that sounded like it came from the very pit of her soul, "No, my lord. You did it for *you.*"

Arthur had heard all about how the pretender Perkin Warbeck and Arthur's cousin Edward Plantagenet had been executed after attempting to escape from the Tower of London.

The news had first come to him in the form of a messenger, then later in whispered gossip among the servants, and finally, from his Aunt Maggie's ashen face.

"Aunt Maggie," he said one morning during their weekly walk, "Would you tell me about your brother?"

The winter chill had claimed the outdoors, snow laying heavily among the castle grounds, but it was the chill between himself and his beloved Aunt Maggie that was causing Arthur deeper distress.

Due to the change in weather, they had taken to wandering the candlelit hallways and enclosed courtyard each week, rather than the garden they frequented during warmer months. And though Arthur would normally look forward to their meetings, over the past few weeks, he couldn't help but feel awkward around her. For nothing he could say or do would help heal her pain.

"He was…" Maggie answered after a moment, her sad eyes staring ahead, though Arthur would wager it wasn't the grey pillars or the stone floor she saw before her, "…happy."

Arthur frowned, "Before?" he clarified.

Maggie nodded, "When we were children, I remember him as always having been happy. He had a lust for life."

She smiled faintly, then went on, "They said he was slow…but it was his imprisonment that led to his lack of development. And no doubt the king believed it useful to say such things about a potential Yorkist claimant –"

She stopped herself, remembering who she was speaking to. But Arthur already knew all about Teddy's supposed underdevelopment. And he had often thought the same, that either way – whether it be true or a lie told to weaken his potential for a worthy alternative to the throne – Teddy's lost mind had been King Henry's doing.

The familiar knot of guilt tightened in Arthur's chest.

"But it matters not," Maggie said, raising her head and sniffing, "He is with God now. He is finally free."

They walked on in silence for a while longer, Arthur hanging his head in shame for what had been done. Though he knew not the extent of how it connected to him and his future.

"I am sorry for your loss, Aunt Maggie," he croaked, when the silence had begun to feel uncomfortable, "I wish he hadn't attempted to escape."

Maggie scoffed then, an involuntary response to the blatant mistruth.

"He did not attempt to escape," she said, her voice quiet but firm. She believed it with all her heart, "Teddy had been placidly imprisoned for over a decade. Why would he suddenly try to escape? And how, if he was so 'slow'? None of it makes any sense."

She shook her head and went on, "No, Arthur. This was about politics. Not treason. The king needed my brother out of the way –"

"My Lady."

Arthur and Maggie jumped at Sir Richard Pole's voice behind them.

"Richard," Maggie said, pressing a palm to her heart, "You frightened us."

He bowed his head at Arthur, "Apologies, Your Grace," then he focused his gaze sharply at his wife, "I trust you are keeping to appropriate conversation?"

It was a hint. One so obvious Arthur couldn't help but pull a face. Was there something Arthur wasn't supposed to know?

"We were discussing the recent traitors' executions," the prince said flatly, to which Maggie stiffened beside him. She would never get used to hearing her docile brother be referred to as a traitor.

Richard nodded, "Troubling times," then to his wife, "Our sons need you, my lady."

Maggie raised one dark eyebrow, fully aware that she was being silenced and even more aware that she could do nothing about it. Anger burned her cheeks and the tips of her ears, and for a moment, she considered standing up to her husband and saying her piece.

But, no. Richard was right. Arthur was under enough strain as it was. He did not need to know that Teddy had only been executed for the sake of securing England's alliance with Spain.

That burden ought only to be carried by his father.

Instead, she looked at Arthur and smiled faintly, saying nothing. And in true regal fashion, the last surviving Plantagenet curtsied to her husband and her prince, then picked up her skirts and left, returning to her Tudor-appointed place in life.

Part 3

The meaning of life is to give life meaning

Chapter 17

September 1500
Ludlow Castle, Shropshire

Since Bernard André's instalment as Arthur's tutor, the prince's Latin was so improved that he was able to compose fluent letters in the beautiful language.

And, at his tutor's suggestion, he used his skills to open communication with his future wife.

"Tell her how you cannot wait to embrace her," Griffith recommended one evening, as the two young men sat privately at the stone chess table in the gardens, the pieces moved to one side and Arthur' quill poised with uncertainty.

"Tell her that she is the light that brightens your dark and gloomy days."

Arthur glanced up from his blank piece of paper, a look of distrust on his face.

"The light to my gloom?" he repeated, his eyebrows quirking, "We have never even met. Surely this is too presumptuous."

Griffith leaned back in his chair with a cheerful sigh, lacing his fingers behind his head.

"Ladies love that kind of imagery. She will find it romantic, trust me."

Arthur frowned and dipped his quill into the ink pot, but his hesitation remained.

Griffith watched his friend. He had changed in recent months, Griffith noted, his face had lost its roundness. But it wasn't just his face which showed signs of manhood. His body, too, had transformed, his limbs having stretched out over the last two summers. He was tall for a boy his age, Griffith thought, as though his body somehow knew that rapid growth had been expected of him his entire life. He was slender but not weak, with a sinewy type of strength about him. But with age, Griffith knew Arthur would one day become a strong leader. Even if his pluck with the ladies was yet at an all-time low.

"You will have to get used to the idea of marriage soon enough, my lord," Griffith said gently and somewhat teasingly, as only a friend could.

Arthur continued to hover his quill over the page. It had already dripped an unseemly black blob on the paper.

"I know," the prince replied without looking up.

Then, with a sigh, he met quill with paper.

Griffith watched, reading the words upside down as Arthur's loopy calligraphy filled the page.

A smile spread over Griffith's face to see Arthur had used his first suggestion, telling the Spanish Princess he could not wait to embrace her.

It was a simple enough – and hopefully truthful – confession. One which would prompt a response from the *infanta* and God willing lead to a less uncomfortable meeting when they were officially married the following year. But Griffith was not sure it would be enough to break down Arthur's walls. Walls Griffith knew he had been building since his early childhood, in order to protect himself from future disappointment.

After a lifetime of being tucked away and separated from his family, never spending enough time with them to ever form a true and meaningful bond; after repeatedly losing beloved nursemaids and tutors at the behest of his father without so much as a goodbye, Arthur had grown to expect being left behind. And with that learned belief, what was the point of forming new connections?

Griffith understood the boy's way of thinking. He had established how to protect himself from further heartache. And although it most likely was not a lesson the king had wished for his heir to learn, it was probably the most engrained message Arthur had obtained.

Ironically, it was something no tutor could ever have taught him any better.

"There," Arthur said after a moment, "Done."

He blew gently onto the paper to dry the ink, then handed it to Griffith.

But Griffith raised his hands, palms facing forward, refusing to take it.

"Oh, no," he said, "That is for your bride's eyes only!" He laughed light-heartedly, "I am certain whatever you have written will do just fine."

Arthur looked down at the three sentences before him, a frown working between his eyebrows.

"I hope you're right."

January 1501
Ludlow Castle, Shropshire

In an effort to dislodge the growing lump of trepidation in his throat, Arthur had ordered for Catalina's portrait from their betrothal be hung up in his chambers facing his bed. That way, her face would be the first thing he would see upon waking and the last upon going to sleep. And surely in time, he would grow accustomed to that very notion, which was so close to coming true.

"The *infanta* is to set sail to England this coming August," Richard Pole reminded the prince one morning, debriefing Arthur as he broke his fast, "The King's Council has drawn up detailed guidelines and timetables for what they intend to happen."

Arthur looked up from his plate of thinly cut meats and cheese, "May I see?"

Pole bristled, "I am not privy to them, Your Grace," he said, "You shall have to ask the king upon our next visit to London."

Arthur breathed a humourless laugh and continued eating, "When would that be? The day *before* my wedding?"

Pole did not respond, knowing all too well that the prince's question was not only sarcastic but also rhetorical. Arthur knew that he was to attend court a month before the special day.

"I can tell you that the princess is to land at Southampton," Richard said, "But until then, your lessons are to continue as per usual. And the king requests that any correspondence with her be made sooner rather than later."

Pole looked down at the letter in his hand then and went on, "The king says, 'Write as your heart sees fit. But if your heart sees fit to write nothing, I request you do not listen.'"

Arthur nodded tiredly, "I do believe I have been told often enough that I am to romance this perfect stranger," he said, "Is it not enough that I am doing all that I can?"

Pole cleared his throat and shifted uncomfortably from one foot to the other.

"If I may be so bold, Your Grace. Have you tried, perhaps, poetry?"

Arthur groaned and waved his hand, dismissing Pole. The older man bowed and quit the room, leaving Arthur alone.

Poetry, sweet words of endearment, none of it felt natural to Arthur, who would much rather speak *honestly* with the girl who would be his queen.

More than anything, he wanted to know what she did for enjoyment. If she took pleasure from playing chess or riding. He'd considered asking her those questions in a letter some weeks prior, but Griffith had rejected the idea.

Girls enjoy embroidery and dancing, he'd said, *I doubt your bride will have much else for an answer.*

So, Arthur had never asked. At least, not directly.

He turned to look at the portrait of Catalina now, where it hung on the wall facing his bed.

"I imagine you enjoy anything that allows you to be outdoors," he said aloud, speaking to the portrait as though she were in the room with him, "I hear your Spanish weather is a lot more agreeable than ours in England."

It had begun one night when Arthur had struggled to fall asleep, twisting and turning under his covers, trying to silence the self-doubt and the nagging voice of his father that often tormented his mind. He had *humphed* angrily onto his back and sat up, ready to call the servant to stoke the fire when his attention had settled onto Catalina's quiet gaze.

"What are you looking at?" he'd snapped in a sharp whisper, and then felt immediately foolish.

But instead of stopping, he went on to apologise to the painting.

"Sorry," he'd mumbled, rubbing a hand over his face with exasperation, "I struggle to sleep sometimes. You'll know all about that soon enough, I guess."

The portrait had stared back, silent, non-judgemental. And before Arthur knew it, he'd lain back on his pillows and just…talked.

Afterwards, it was as if his chest had opened up and he could breathe easier. As though voicing all his concerns, fears, and wonderments aloud had somehow halved their weight. Spoken out loud, they did not seem quite so intimidating.

He'd taken to speaking to Catalina's portrait whenever he was alone, whenever he felt like the weight of the world was crushing him.

It soothed him somehow. Even though Arthur knew it did not aid their true rapport, he felt himself relaxing at the mere sight of her. Her calm expression, her blue compassionate eyes, they had a way of quietening the insecurities swirling about in his mind.

Presently, he rose from his seat at the table – his stomach too knotted to allow him to finish his breakfast – and stood before the painting.

He released a long sigh and stretched his neck from side to side as he looked up at it.

"Perhaps Griffith is right," he told Catalina's gentle regard, "Maybe you will be the light to my dark and gloom."
The princess' likeness answered in silence. And Arthur nodded to himself before turning to leave the room.

"Either that, or I shall surely die of boredom with this life."

Chapter 18

<u>1501</u>

The Spanish Princess' journey to England was anything but straightforward.

Catalina de Aragon and her entourage left Corunna in Spain, as agreed, on the 17th of August 1501, but shortly after their departure, a massive storm forced her ships to return to the port of Laredo for repairs and the arrival of favourable weather.

Upon hearing this news, Henry VII – who had become increasingly paranoid over the years that this union would fall through – sent out master mariners and pilots familiar with the routes to Spain to search for the *infanta's* fleet. To his great relief, they were able to locate the princess' ships and guide them towards England a few days later.

But that was only the beginning of the princess' struggles to reach London.

For months in advance, King Henry had arranged for the princess' ships to arrive at Southampton, where a magnificent formal reception had been organised to greet her. However, due to further complications at sea, the Spanish ships were guided to land at Plymouth instead, where they finally arrived on the 2nd of October, weeks after their intended entrance.

"I have sent Lord Willoughby to welcome the princess with as much dignity as is possible after she has landed over a hundred miles further west than expected!" the king declared in frustration.

He was pacing up and down before his throne in the great hall, too antsy to sit. His mother and wife were standing before him, their concerned expressions mirroring the other's.

"Willoughby is an excellent organiser," Margaret Beaufort said, attempting to settle her son, who she knew was on tenterhooks about this deviation, "He has taken a team of ceremonial experts and seasoned knights. The princess will be made most welcome." But the princess' arrival at the wrong place was not the end of what would go awry, the party taking much longer than expected to achieve the capital. And by early November, King Henry had reached the end of his patience, annoyed by the natural and human delays to the schedule he had so carefully planned.

"Send word to my heir to meet with me at the hunting lodge near Dogmersfield," Henry told his messenger as he pulled on his riding gloves.

"What is happening, my lord?" Lizzie asked, standing from her seat at the window, her ladies following suit.

Henry looked over at her, appearing angelic with the light coming in through the window behind her.

"I must see her with my own eyes," he replied.

5th November 1501
Bishop's Palace, Dogmersfield

Father and son arrived at Dogmersfield – where the *infanta* and her entourage had stopped to rest – in the late hours of the 5th of November.

But to Arthur's great relief, for he had been riding all day and was covered in mud and sweat, the king had instructed they spend the night and freshen up before meeting his bride in the morning.

6th November 1501
Bishop's Palace, Dogmersfield

Catalina de Aragon was resting in her chamber, her lady, Lina de Cardonnes, hovering about quietly as she tidied away the princess' dress and veil, when suddenly rushed footsteps were heard approaching, followed by an unseemly banging on the door.

"This is the king!" came a holler in English, then again in Latin. Catalina sat upright, covering herself with her slender arms as though the man could see her in her nightgown through the locked door.

"I have travelled with the intention of making an assessment of the princess with my own eyes!" called the king, banging again when the door was not immediately opened, "I request an audience!"

Frightened, Catalina looked up at Lina, who now held a robe open before her. The princess rose from the bed and allowed herself to be wrapped in the crimson garb while one of her other ladies placed a veil and coronet over her head.

"This is most improper!" Catalina called through the closed door in Latin as her ladies readied her as quickly as they could, "I shall write to my father of this!"

And yet the princess had little choice but to receive the king.

After all, she was in his land now. And no matter how uncouth their customs seemed to her, she would have to get used to them.

Lina opened the door after casting one final glance at her mistress and assessing her as suitable enough to meet the king – as suitable as she could be given the rush – and in stormed a dishevelled and rather irked-looking, grey-haired man in his mid-forties.

As her ladies dipped curtsies all around her, Catalina stood bone straight. She would not show respect to this man who clearly had none for her.

He wore a crown on his head and riding clothes stitched with gold and embroidered with the Tudor rose. But despite his external display, Catalina was not impressed.

"Forgive me," he mumbled then, as though suddenly realising his lack of decorum, "But I wished only to see what we have so long been waiting for."

Catalina raised her chin higher, defiant, "You see now," she said.

But Henry breathed a small laugh, "Will you remove the veil, perhaps?"

Catalina visibly stiffened, "I cannot. Not until I stand with Prince Arthur before God."

Henry nodded, his mouth twitching with annoyance.

"Very well," he said nonetheless, "If you wish not to show me, perhaps you will allow my son to lay his eyes on you when you meet later today."

Catalina gasped, "Today?"

Henry nodded, "We have both ridden hard, eager to meet you, Your Grace. I suggest you ready yourself to meet your husband."

"He is not yet my husband," Catalina replied sharply as the king began to leave.

"You were married by proxy," Henry replied, that familiar paranoia he had begun to feel about this union spiking in his veins, "By law, he is your husband. Is he not?"

Catalina could not deny it, for a lump had formed in her throat.

But the king was right. By law, she and Arthur were already married. Though they had never even met.

She knew this, of course. But the King of England's forced entrance into her chambers had alarmed her, and she had wanted to regain some control, even if only in words.

After all, she was the daughter of the two mightiest Catholic rulers in all the world. She would not be made to feel like a wilted flower in this damp and grey land.

Later that morning, the king and his heir stood facing each other by the fire, Henry's hands clamped firmly on Arthur's shoulders.

"You must woo her, son," he said intensely, "I have only spoken to her briefly, but she appears to have a fiery temperament."

A smile formed as Henry spoke the words. He was not opposed to a strong woman. In fact, she reminded him a little of his own lovely wife.

"I will do my best to please you, Lord Father," Arthur replied.

"Not to please *me*, son! Do your best to please your bride!"
Arthur nodded.

"Of course," he said, though Arthur knew it was one and the same. If he managed to make his wife happy, his father would be happy.
Half an hour later, Arthur and Henry were led to the princess' chambers, and Arthur began to feel more and more embarrassed at his father's crude entry into her private rooms.
Would she think badly of him for how his father had acted?
Had his father already muddied the waters between them before Arthur had even said a word to her?
The guard opened the door to the *infanta's* chamber and King Henry stepped inside. Arthur followed, his chest feeling tight and heavy.
But when he laid eyes upon the statuesque princess standing by the window, her golden-red hair curling out along the bottom of her veil, Arthur's anxiety evaporated. For though he had not yet properly seen her face in the flesh, thanks to his better acquaintance with her portrait, he felt like he already knew her.

They supped together that evening, surrounded by a small party of English noblemen and women, and the princess' ladies.
The Spanish minstrels played merry tunes, and a small dance party twirled cheerfully once the plates were cleared.
Arthur and Catalina sat side by side watching the performance, both smiling faintly but neither of them willing to break the silence with mundane words. There was plenty of time for that, and Arthur would prefer to get to know his bride without dozens of eyes observing their every move or straining to hear every word.
The next morning, Arthur bowed gallantly at Catalina before he and his party departed towards London in preparation for the imminent wedding.

Catalina would follow the next day, to give them time to announce her grand entrance.

<u>10th November 1501</u>
<u>London</u>

"She is magnificent," Arthur said with a contented sigh as he and his mother stood by the large window overlooking the city, watching the princess' grand arrival into London.
He could not see her, of course, for they were too far away from the river, where her entry had been planned as a wondrous river pageant.
Lizzie looked at her eldest son. Her firstborn. The boy she had created with her own body, who she loved fiercely but who she hardly knew.
"Your father tells me she has not yet removed her veil?" she said.
Arthur nodded, "I do not speak of her appearance, Lady Mother. Though we already know from her portrait that she is fair. I speak of her demeanour, of her grace."
Lizzie looked away, following her son's calm gaze over the palace gardens and the city beyond, "She will be a good wife to you. And a good queen. She has been raised for it."
Arthur stiffened at that, rattled suddenly by his mother's statement, though he didn't know what else he had expected from her.
"Yes," he said cooly, his former contentment dashed, "She and I have long been set on this path, have we not?"
Lizzie nodded slowly, unaware of her son's change in disposition, "You are each other's destinies."
Arthur's eyes narrowed slightly as he considered his mother's chosen words.

"It is not 'destiny', Lady Mother," Arthur said, surprising himself with his candour, "Fate had absolutely no part to play in this union."

Lizzie opened her mouth to answer, a look of concern twisting her face, but Arthur turned away from her and from the view, suddenly irked by the whispers of cheery calls blowing in the wind.

Arthur left the room, angry at himself for forgetting his place in the world. He had been born for a political purpose, not for happiness, and he ought not to get his hopes up.

"It is not fated if mere men rolled the dice."

Chapter 19

<u>14th November 1501</u>
<u>St Paul's Cathedral, London</u>

   Arthur was getting married.
Not betrothed, not married by proxy. Officially, legitimately getting married. And yet he felt like he was in some sort of dream, like he was not in control of his own body.
Which, in some way, he wasn't.
King Henry VII intended for this wedding to be the wedding of the century, and from what Arthur could tell as he made his way towards the Cathedral on horseback, his father had spent extravagantly to achieve that goal.
London was decorated with beautiful tapestries, some depicting scenes from the Bible, others classical stories and even military history. Royal badges decorated the buildings near the cathedral, including Tudor Roses, white stags, and the Beaufort portcullis.
The streets were thronged with people, many having travelled from afar to catch a glimpse of their future king and queen, and they were all – lords and servants alike – dressed in their best liveries. They cheered and waved as Arthur glided past, majestic on his white steed. Some even threw flowers. Arthur caught one midair and nodded his head in thanks at the crowd before dismounting when he reached the cathedral.
Inside, Arthur was not surprised to see a full congregation. Nobles, lords, ladies, ambassadors from all over Europe, they had all come to witness this momentous occasion.
He walked slowly up towards the altar, and as he did so he noticed that the staff had put all the gold, jewels and relics out on display. He smiled faintly and shook his head. Of course they

had. Nothing was too good for the king's son. Except, perhaps, some genuine human connection.

The Archbishop of Canterbury nodded at Arthur in greeting and Arthur nodded back, inhaling deeply to steady himself for what would be a long day.

He had made his entrance to much excited muttering and enthusiastic grinning. But as soon as the trumpets sounded to announce his bride's arrival outside the cathedral, everyone's focus fell to the princess.

And when she stepped onto the red carpet on the walkway, Arthur understood why.

She wore a pleated, Spanish style dress of white satin embroidered with pearls and stitched with gold thread. A white veil bordered with gold and precious stones covered her face and hair, which hung loosely down her back in auburn waves. And though Arthur still could not properly see her face, as she approached, he could faintly make out the round outline of her rosy cheeks and the intense yet nervous stare of her eyes.

She was a sight to behold, and the crowd was right to focus solely on her.

Prince Harry, who had walked Catalina down the aisle, took her hand from the crook of his elbow and delivered her to Arthur. He thanked Harry with a quick smile, to which the ten-year-old replied with a shameless grin and a wink. Arthur pressed his lips together. It was all he could do not to laugh at the bold prince.

The nuptial mass lasted for three hours, the Archbishop of Canterbury uniting England and Spain with much ceremony and tradition.

As he droned on, Arthur could not help but steal glances at his bride. It was the closest they had ever been, and despite knowing he was only privy to her presence because of their father's colluding, Arthur was enchanted by her proximity.

She smelt of cinnamon and apples, he thought, and he unintentionally leant closer as they knelt side by side before the archbishop, forgetting for a second that the whole world was watching them with bated breath.

Then it was time, the moment in which he would finally lay eyes on his bride, not through a veil or via a portrait, but in the flesh. He turned to her – this stranger who was that instant made his wife – and peeled the shroud from over her face.

And what he saw underneath was far beyond anything he could ever have imagined.

<u>Baynard's Castle, London</u>

Due to the couples' young age – Arthur fifteen and Catalina sixteen – they were not expected to consummate their marriage during the bedding ceremony, which took place on the eve of their wedding day.

Instead, the bishop merely blessed the marriage bed while the couple lay stiffly underneath the blankets, the crowd of noble lords and ladies surrounding them as witnesses.

But soon enough, when the bishop concluded his mumbling, the onlookers emptied out, leaving the young newlyweds alone for the very first time.

Arthur lay on his back, his arms tucked at his sides underneath the blanket, feeling extremely aware of every one of his limbs and their distance from hers. He felt warm. Not sickly or unwell, but warm with nervousness. As though his skin needed to remind him that it was there.

If he were anything like Griffith, he may have edged closer and lain a hand on hers, maybe looked into her eyes and smiled before kissing her gently on the lips.

But he was not like Griffith, and instead he allowed the silence to grow wider and deeper, until the mere thought of breaking it seemed physically impossible.

From the corner of his eye, he could see that she too lay on her back, her hands over her chest, her fingers picking and pulling at each other with – what? Nervousness?

He frowned. Was she just as ill at ease as he?

He inhaled to steady himself. It was up to him to make the first move.

Ever so slowly, he detached his hand from where it had frozen in place underneath the blanket, and reached out his pinkie finger until it gently grazed her side – an attempt at closing the tense gap between them.

She flinched at his touch, and Arthur snatched his hand away, immediately wishing he hadn't crossed that line.

Humiliated, his cheeks burning brightly, he turned his back on her and shuffled as closely to the edge of the mattress as he dared without falling off, eager to gain as much distance between him and his wife as he could.

He stared at the fire in the corner, more mortified than he had ever been in his entire life, and he longed for the quiet seclusion of Ludlow, regardless that it had once felt like purgatory. For this – this nauseating feeling of embarrassment – was surely hell.

15th November 1501

The following day, Arthur awoke before the dawn. He'd had a fitful sleep, the sound of laughter and mockery echoing in the depths of his subconscious following the previous night's failure. Turning over carefully so as not to alert her of his wakefulness, Arthur noticed with great relief that Catalina was still asleep, and he crept out of the bed as silently as he could.

Passing guards and servants as they made their early morning rounds readying the castle, Arthur slipped out into the courtyard, desperate for a gulp of fresh air after a night of stifling his breaths. He sucked in the sweet morning breeze through his nose and expelled it out of his mouth in an effort to lighten his heavy chest.

He shook his head. It seemed he would sooner let himself suffocate than confront his insecurities.

Arthur groaned under his breath and pressed his palms tightly over his eyes in frustration. At himself. At his father. At the world he was born into.

What kind of a young prince was he that he didn't gratefully accept the marvellous gift that was given to him?

He had it all at his fingertips. A beautiful wife, the throne of England, the *world*, if he wanted it.

It wasn't that it wasn't enough. The feeling that weighed him down was not one of disappointment. Lord knew he was as privileged as could be!

So then why couldn't he be grateful? Why was his conscience putting up so much resistance?

He knew why. Though he felt pathetic to even admit it.

It was too much. It was *all* too much.

And he wasn't sure for how much longer he could carry the future of England on his own before his body and mind gave out.

Arthur returned indoors but resolved to wander the less occupied areas of the castle.

He knew he was being evasive, but he told himself he was but exploring Baynard. After all, he didn't often get the opportunity to leave Ludlow Castle.

After a while, when the sun had risen beyond the horizon and he knew the courtiers would be up and about, he steered clear of the great hall where most of the court would be, and instead decided to risk returning to his royal apartments. Surely by now, the princess would have risen to present herself to the king and queen – as he himself ought to do.

But he could not bring himself to face her. Not yet. Not when the humiliation of the previous night still rang loudly in his mind.

He took the risk, and as expected, his chambers were empty – save for a servant stoking the fire. Arthur slipped inside, beelining to the cushioned seat by the window where he'd left his Bible. He made himself comfortable and cracked open the well-worn book, eager to immerse himself into its comforting words and attempting to forget what irked his cluttered brain.

"Oh, Arthur."
Arthur looked up at the sound of his mother's voice. It was but an hour later, and he had been discovered.
"Why do I find you here and not in the hall getting to know your new wife?" his mother asked, entering the room and closing the door behind her.
Arthur imagined her ladies standing idly outside, not knowing what to do without their mistress.
He dropped the book and sighed.
"We have nothing in common," he said, unwilling to admit to his own shortcomings, "It was easier to talk to her through letters when she was miles away in Spain."
And when she was no more than a portrait, Arthur thought secretively.
Lizzie sat down beside her son and cupped his pale cheek with her hand, "You will stumble over conversation to begin with, as is natural," she said, "Your father and I went through the same. But look at us now, completely devoted to one another and with four incredible children to show for it."
Arthur's stomach dropped at the memory of his lost siblings, the ones who had not survived infancy. First baby Elizabeth and then baby Edmund, who Arthur had never even met.
He thought he noticed a sadness cross his mother's face for a moment, perhaps also thinking of the children she had lost, perhaps thinking she ought to have said '*six* incredible children'. He wondered if she felt guilty for choosing not to mention them. Or if she was guarding her heart by keeping them locked in there.
"You must be the one to make the effort, my son," she said then, returning his mind to the present, "The *infanta* has left behind her entire life, left all she has ever known and just this morning given up her birth name, for this union."
Arthur frowned at the news.
Lizzie nodded, "She is to be known as Katherine from now on."

Arthur looked pensively at the stone floor.

She has anglicised her name, he thought, then chuckled underneath his breath at the memory of him telling Griffith he may refer to him as Arthur instead of Your Grace, the 'anglicised' version. Of course, he knew now that the word did not mean 'easier'. In fact, Arthur realised then, if anything, leaving her true name in the past, along with everything else she'd ever known, was surely anything but easy.

"I quite liked her name. Catalina," he admitted, wondering for the first time how his wife must be feeling in this foreign land and being lumbered with a husband who couldn't even touch her without fleeing the first moment he got.

Shame stabbed at his heart – yet another thing to feel inadequate about.

December 1501

"What is wrong with her, Arthur?" Griffith asked his friend one evening, after Arthur confided in him how utterly bewildered he felt.

They were playing a game of chess in Arthur's rooms, a moment of solitary peace from the Christmastide and wedding festivities. But Arthur's mind wasn't in the game, and at Griffith's question, he rose from his seat with a groan.

"Nothing!" he grumbled, running a hand down his face, "My God, will no one ever understand me?"

He'd muttered the question to himself, but Griffith had heard.

"Explain it to me," he said, leaning back in his chair and linking his fingers behind his head, "What, exactly, is the issue?"

Arthur sighed with exasperation, "I have already told you. I do not know *how* to explain it. It's like – it's as if –" he licked his dry lips, his blue eyes wide with adrenaline, "It's *too much*, it's all just too much! I feel as though I am being watched. Constantly! Like every step I take is measured, every word I say is analysed…"

He pinched the bridge of his nose and squeezed his eyes shut in frustration, "You won't understand. No one will."

But Griffith's mouth twitched at the sides and he nodded, "You're right. I don't understand. From where I'm standing you have it all –"

"But that's it!" Arthur bellowed, interrupting his friend with a rancour Griffith was not used to seeing in the young prince, "That is *exactly* it! I have it all, it is all available to me. But it's too much! I am not ready! I'm not worthy! Who decided I should have it all? God?"

Griffith's brows scrunched into a questioning expression, "Well, yes…"

Arthur shook his head, "I don't want it. But I cannot ever admit to any of this! *Lord,* do you know how good it feels to finally *say* it out loud?"

But then the exhilarated look in the prince's eyes morphed into fear, and he slumped back down at the chess table, facing Griffith.

"You know you cannot ever tell my father – or anyone – about what I have said."

Griffith nodded, "You can trust me."

Arthur swallowed, searching his friend's face for a hint of disloyalty. But he found none. And for a moment, he wondered if perhaps he would prefer it if Griffith *did* tell his father. Let the burden of England fall to his brother Harry instead…

But he shook his head free of that poisonous thought. He wouldn't wish this burden onto anyone.

Arthur dropped his head in his hands and let out a ragged exhale.

"It does not matter," he said, "I have to get over this hurdle, and I will. I just need some more time."

The two young men sat in silence for a while following Arthur's outburst, both staring into the crackling fire beside them as it ate away at the logs, turning them to ash.

"I believe I know how I can help you," Griffith said after a moment, a slow grin spreading over his lips.

Arthur gave him his full attention, though his eyes were hooded and impassive. He didn't have much faith in whatever plan his friend had in mind.

"What if someone recognises me?" Arthur protested but an hour later, as he stood huddled and cloaked outside the brothel Griffith had dragged him to.
Griffith smirked, "Keep your hood over your head," he said, before disappearing into the stew.
Arthur blinked after him, equal parts disturbed and rapt by how nonchalantly Griffith had entered the establishment. As leisurely as entering the gardens at Ludlow.
He must grace these places with his presence often for it to be so easy.
Arthur looked over his shoulder, then groaned under his breath before begrudgingly following his friend inside.
It was warm but dimly lit, and Arthur had to squint to try and identify Griffith among the other bodies moving about. The acrid smell of sweat and Lord knew what else entered Arthur's nostrils, and he pulled a face.
He was able to spot Griffith easily, however, for after a moment, Arthur realised that he and Griffith were the only ones fully dressed.
Arthur clenched his jaw and moved through the poorly lit chambers towards him, trying to ignore the moaning and groaning coming from behind closed doors.
"This," Griffith said as Arthur approached, presenting him with a beautiful redhead, "Is Margery."
She was bare-breasted and smiling. And from Griffith's grin Arthur knew that he'd had her. She was lovely, there was no denying that. Smooth, pale skin that glinted in the candlelight, two pink nipples just begging to be admired. But the thought of touching her did not appeal to Arthur, and he felt only burning shame at the prospect.

He looked from Margery to Griffith, unable to comprehend how he had gotten here. How his admission of overwhelming stress had led him to this bleak place.

"Excuse me," Arthur muttered then, turning around and heading out the door.

His stomach churned at the thought of that woman's body being repeatedly used for the pleasures of men, and as he took in large gulps of the cold night air, a rush of pity for Margery and the others in that hovel behind him hummed in his veins.

Suddenly, his own life did not seem quite so burdensome.

"Was that your plan all along?" Arthur said aloud, when he heard Griffith's footsteps behind him, "To show me the struggles of the common folk?"

Griffith sighed, his breath misting before him, "No. My plan was for you to explore the many beautiful things in life that can't be learned from a book."

Arthur looked at Griffith, his eyes narrowed as he attempted to decipher his tone.

But then a smile twitched at Griffith's lips, and the two men chuckled under their breaths.

"Come on, Your Grace," Griffith said, clapping Arthur companionably on the shoulder, "If your father finds out I took you out of the castle grounds, he'll throw me in the Tower."

Arthur's brief glee quickly dispersed at the mention of the king, "Yes," he said solemnly, "My father."

Griffith clicked his tongue as they walked, "You know. Just because you were born into royalty and have all the gold and silver you could ever want, does not mean your struggles are any less real."

Arthur laughed humourlessly, "They do not measure up to that though, do they?" he asked rhetorically, waving his hand behind them.

Griffith shrugged, the corners of his mouth pulling down at the sides, "I don't know," he said, "Maybe not. But regardless of what life we've been given, we – *all* – have our own crosses to bear. What may seem like a small thing to one, can be a big thing to another. Your frets are just as real as anyone else's. It's about how you decide to deal with them that matters. And what you choose to do with the life that was given to you."

Chapter 20

<u>January 1502</u>
<u>Ludlow Castle, Shropshire</u>

Griffith's words rang in Arthur's ears.

And yet he could not simply overcome years of engrained insecurities just because he wanted to.

But there was hope. For shortly after the Christmastide celebrations, Arthur and his new bride were sent to his home at Ludlow, away from the court and its prying eyes, where the young couple would surely get to know one another better. The beginning of what would hopefully be a wonderful partnership.

Arthur awoke that first morning back at Ludlow with the knowledge that he had only one challenge for the foreseeable future, and that was to forge some kind of relationship with his wife.

Lessons had been put aside at the order of his father in favour of this one task, the future of England depending far more on his successful marriage to the Spanish Princess than on anything else. And so, after washing with rosewater and dressing in a fine velvet jacket and matching hose, Arthur stood before the princess' door and exhaled slowly to calm his nerves. Then he knocked on the door and waited to be admitted.

"Yes?" came her voice, and Arthur turned the doorknob.

Katherine stood by the fireplace, her eyes wide and her cheeks pink as she clutched a fur around her shoulders.

"My lord," she said, curtsying at the sight of him.

Arthur realised that he had often seen the princess near the hearth back in London, too. And he thought her Spanish blood must not yet be used to the cold English weather.

There was a plate of unfinished food on the table beside her, and he cleared his throat awkwardly. Had he interrupted her breakfast? Was their English food bland compared to what she had left behind?

But instead of asking either of those questions, Arthur's mouth betrayed him.

"My father ordered that I make more of an effort."

It was true. Before their departure, King Henry had pulled his son aside and requested he stop acting as though this were a chore, as though he and his mother hadn't obtained him one of the most beautiful princesses in Europe. Arthur had nodded and tried to ignore his father's obvious disappointment in him. Clearly, he – and no doubt the whole court – had borne witness to Arthur's shortcomings as a prince, as a young man.

He shook his head at himself, "Please," he said, hoping to fix his misstep, "Eat," and he took a seat at the head of the table.

They sat in silence, Katherine picking at the cheese and cuts of meat on her plate while Arthur watched the flames, his mind searching for a topic they could discuss.

"Are you enjoying it here?" he said suddenly, the stillness having grown heavy around them. He'd needed to say *something*.

The princess blinked, "I have not had the chance to explore much in the short time we have been here…"

Arthur shook his head, "No, no," he said, frowning, "Here, as in, England."

"Oh…" Katherine breathed, then licked her lips as she organized her thoughts, "Yes, very much so."

Arthur nodded, unsure if she was telling the truth.

He watched her as she looked down at her hands, unable suddenly to meet his eye. It was the first time he considered the possibility that she, too, did not know what to say to him.

And in some strange burst of compassion, he leant forward and confided in her, "I spoke to you before you arrived," he said, "Not to you directly, of course, but…to your portrait."

Katherine blushed, "You did?" she said, a small smile tugging at her lips. He looked at them.

"What did you say?" she asked, lifting her gaze from her lap to meet his.

His cheeks burned all of a sudden, flustered to have been caught watching her mouth. He blinked in quick succession, shook his head.

"Just mundane things," he admitted with a small laugh, "Just to ease the tension for when you arrived."

Katherine shifted in her seat, "And did it?" she asked, "Ease the tension?"

Arthur grinned despite himself, "No," he admitted, looking away, "No, not really. When I first saw you at Dogmersfield, I thought it had. But…"

Katherine nodded knowingly, "We have time to get to know one another," she said, "But knowing we are both as…apprehensive…as the other…I believe that is a good first step."

Arthur smiled gratefully across the table at her. For of course she was right. They had all the time in the world.

<u>March 1502</u>

It was a bright morning, the warmest since Katherine's arrival, and Arthur imagined she would be glad to see the end of her first English winter.

She was breakfasting in the garden. He could hear her and her ladies chattering among themselves, her gentle laughter whirling in through the open window of his chambers.

Resting his elbows on the stone parapet, he watched them for a moment, and though he could not hear of what they spoke, he noticed a smile had started to take shape on his face simply to hear the sound of Katherine's voice.

Since their mutual admission of unease, Arthur had felt himself relaxing in her company. Granted they did not often spend much time together – his duties as Prince of Wales meaning he was often busy with his Privy Council – but on the odd occasion where their schedules *did* align, Arthur no longer felt compelled to hide away, but rather, he found himself looking forward to spending time with her. Even if only to sit in companionable silence.

"My lady!" he called from the balcony then, surprising not only the three ladies below him but even himself.
They looked up, shielding their eyes from the sun, and Arthur's chest soared to see his wife grinning prettily at the sight of him.

"Do you wish to sup with me tonight?" he called, cupping one hand around his mouth.
Katherine pursed her lips in a way that suggested she was holding in her delight, and even from the small distance between them, Arthur was sure he could see a twinkle in her eyes.

"My lady will be there!" one of Katherine's ladies – *Lina, was it?* – called back, to which the other one giggled into her hand while Katherine continued to beam up at Arthur.
He nodded once, sealing the agreement.

"Until then!" he called. Then he pushed himself off the parapet, feeling energised for the day ahead.

That evening, as Arthur's groom closed the clasp on his shirt sleeve and stepped back to allow the prince a full view of himself in the mirror, Griffith articulated the very thought that was also on Arthur's mind.

"You think you're ready?"
Arthur inhaled as he observed his reflection, then nodded his head 'yes'. But a small voice in his head dared to say 'no'.
Griffith clapped him on the back and grinned devilishly, "You won't forget this night, Arthur," he said, "Tonight, you shall be in Spain."

Arthur stood by the fireplace when Katherine entered his chambers, half his face glowing orange as he turned to welcome her in with a friendly smile.
She looked beautiful, he thought. Far more so than on the day of their wedding. More so than in the portrait he had once so admired.

"My lord," she said in greeting as she bobbed a quick curtsy.

Arthur stepped towards her, welcoming her, "There's no more need for that here," he said, "When it is just us, we are equals."

Us.

It felt good to say the word, so loaded with the promise of their future.

"Come," Arthur said then, waving his hand towards the table at the centre of the large room, laid with many dishes of roasted meats, pies and pastries.

The couple took their seats, and while the servants began to dish out servings of all the delicacies, Arthur glanced in Katherine's direction. She appeared at ease, and it loosened Arthur's knotted shoulders slightly.

"Katherine," he said once the servants had retreated to the shadows.

She hesitated for a moment, "Arthur," she replied playfully when he didn't immediately continue.

He smiled at the sound of his name on her lips, finding the undertone of doubt in her voice as she addressed him so informally endearing.

"Tell me about your home," he said, having been eager to hear about her country for some time, "Do you miss it?"

Katherine smiled uncertainly down at her plate, "I do," she admitted, "I do miss it. But England is my home now. I have accepted that."

Arthur nodded, "But the Alhambra," he said, hoping to coax her into giving him some information, "I hear it is very grand."

Katherine chuckled then.

"Yes, the Alhambra," she said, rolling her tongue at the 'r', the word sounding completely different to how Arthur had pronounced it, "it is very grand."

Arthur's cheeks flushed scarlet at his mishap, but Katherine went on, sighing, "What I miss the most are the colours."

Arthur frowned, looking around at the vibrant red tapestries hanging on the walls, the rich browns of the table and chairs, the glittering golds and blues of the rugs.

Katherine, noticing him looking, explained further.

"In Spain, in the Alhambra, the walls are decorated with tiles and jewels of all pigments. The waters run clear and pure, and the gardens are always in abundance," she looked around herself, "One thing I have noticed is just how grey England can appear."

"It is the season," Arthur answered monotonously, a little defensive of his country, "Winters can be quite wet and bleak here. But spring is around the corner. And with it, the colours will return."

Katherine smiled politely at Arthur, "I do not wish to offend."

"You do not," he replied, though he had felt a pinch of it.

They ate in silence, Arthur feeling the atmosphere shifting slightly the longer neither of them spoke. But he did not know what else to say, his earlier attempt at conversation having led to a dead end.

When they were done and the servants cleared the table, Arthur turned to his groom and whispered something to him, before walking around the table and towards Katherine.

He had one more trick up his sleeve before he called it a night.

"Do you wish to dance?" he asked, offering his hand.

She looked up at him, hesitating for but a second before nodding and taking his hand.

But that one moment was enough for Arthur to understand that she was not ready for anything further to happen tonight. Not when they hadn't so much as shared a dance before this very moment.

And though Arthur hadn't wanted to admit it before – when he was blinded by the growing feelings of excitement and fondness in his chest – in truth, neither was he.

The following week, Arthur awoke from a dream where he and Katherine had been surrounded by young children as they strolled leisurely through the palace gardens, the summer sun warming their faces.

The dream had been as brief as a whisper, but the warmth of Katherine's hand in his and the sound of children's laughter echoed through into his consciousness, leaving behind a profound sense of achievement.

Perhaps he and Katherine would find happiness in their future after all.

But it would never come to be if he did not act.

With the sweet residual wisps of his dreams spurring him on, Arthur dressed quickly, his groom aiding him with the more finicky parts of the attire.

He found Katherine and her ladies playing cards in the hall, one of her ladies laughing loudly as Katherine told them something in Spanish, their cards held close to their chests to keep them secret.

"My lady," Arthur said as he approached, maintaining eye contact for a moment longer than he would have dared but the previous day, "May I join you for a game?"

Katherine blinked, "Of—of course, Your Grace."

They took their seats opposite one another, her ladies retreating to the window in the far corner of the hall to give them some privacy.

"How do you fair at *primero*?" Arthur asked as he dealt out the cards.

Katherine smiled and shrugged casually, playing coy, "You will have to find out."

They arranged their cards and took their turns, Arthur feeling the tension in his shoulders melting away as they played, like ice turning to water in the spring.

After a moment, Arthur laid down his cards.

"I win," he said, and watched as she leant forward to examine his hand.

She sighed through her nose to realise her defeat, and when she looked up to meet his gaze, he did not look away.

Not because he knew he shouldn't, but, strangely, because he didn't want to.

She smiled lightly at him, "Do you care for another round?"

He did not reply, and in the fleeting silence, Katherine tentatively licked her lips, causing his gaze to briefly drop to her mouth.

Arthur noticed her take in a shaky breath, a slight yet undeniable reaction, and it was like something inside him came alive.

Before he could stop himself, Arthur rose from his seat and leant over the games table, thrilled to see that Katherine was leaning towards him, too.

And then, without pomp or ceremony, they kissed.

Chapter 21

1st April 1502
Ludlow Castle, Shropshire

The wind howled outside, rattling the wooden shutters like bones. The previous month's promise of warmth had been revoked in favour of April showers and an unseasonably cold breeze, the cool and damp clinging tightly onto the stone walls of the castle.

But it was the storm within the castle which would rock all of England, for Prince Arthur and his Spanish Princess had fallen deathly ill.

"There is nothing more any of us can do," the bearded physician informed Griffith after backing away from the prince's bed, his quick examination concluded. It seemed not even the professionals wished to get too close, "It is the Sweat…"

Griffith, who stood at a careful distance by the door, nodded vaguely at the old man as he pushed past.

"Only prayer can save the prince now!" the physician called over his shoulder, his robes flapping behind him in his haste.

Maggie and Richard Pole entered then, their faces as fear stricken as no doubt Griffith's was.

"Any news?" Maggie asked, stopping regrettably beside Griffith, though he knew she would've wanted to be by Arthur's side, holding his hand.

Griffith shook his head, and all three looked towards their gentle prince.

Arthur lay, pale-faced and drenched in sweat, beneath many blankets of wool and linen. The physicians had advised to keep him covered, to draw out the sweat. But in his subconscious anguish, Arthur would thrash them off more often than anyone dared to approach him. After another fitful spasm, the physician had settled the blankets over the prince before he'd left, but

Griffith could tell from how badly Arthur was shaking that they would soon be on the floor once again.

"His skin is the colour of paper," Griffith heard Maggie whisper, as though scared to admit aloud what they were all thinking: that it was a vast contrast to his once flushed vigour of youth.

But it wasn't just Arthur who had fallen prey to the mysterious disease, for across the castle in her own chambers, Princess Katherine, too, writhed about in pain in her sleep, her Spanish ladies utterly flummoxed as to how to heal her from this mysterious English disease.

The pair remained unconscious all that first night of April, sometimes calling out in their restless sleep or groaning in pain, but otherwise silent as the dead.

That is, until the sky cleared and the sun rose over the horizon, bringing with it hope for a new dawn.

2nd April 1502

Arthur lay, his mind caged by his dying body, as the rest of the Prince's Court bustled about in a panic, unable to do anything to help but unwilling to admit defeat.

For surely, God would not take away so suddenly what he had been crafting to perfection for the past fifteen years.

But somehow, in the deepest pits of his subconscious, Arthur knew better. And after all this time, his antipathy towards his future as King of England finally made sense.

Perhaps he had always known, on some intuitive level, that he would never achieve the throne. Perhaps that was why he could never envision himself sitting upon it.

He was dying. That much he knew for certain.

And no amount of praying, hoping, bargaining, waiting, sweating would save him from his fate.

For *this* was his fate.

Not what his mother and father had hoped for him, not what his grandmother had prayed for, not what Aunt Maggie and Teddy had sacrificed for. All that was but insignificant human interference in God's greater plan. For only He could rule on people's destinies, no matter how much great men chose to believe that they had a say in it.

A moment of consciousness, a tiny sliver of light as he attempted to open his eyes.
He quickly closed them again when the glare hurt his head, like a knife piercing his skull
"It is too bright…"
He heard movement then, frantic rustling of fabric as someone jumped into action at his mutterings, and the sweet scent of apples and cinnamon graced his senses.
"Katherine…?" Arthur mumbled, hoping he wasn't dreaming. That would be too cruel.
"I am here," he heard her whisper, and then he felt her take his hand.
Arthur smiled, despite everything, all the pain, all the discomfort, all the dreaded realisations.
"I dreamed of the Alhambra…" he breathed, barely above a whisper.
But Katherine had heard him. She was closer than any physician or dear friend ventured to go. As a survivor, Katherine was certain she was safe from the infamous *Sudor Anglicus*.
"What did you see in your dream?" Katherine whispered back, a flicker of hope rekindling in her still-weakened chest.
Perhaps her young husband would recover after all. Just as she had.
Arthur smiled faintly, though his eyes remained closed. Katherine imagined he could still see glimpses of his colourful vision.
"We were walking…our fingers were brushing the bejewelled walls," he coughed then, a deep, wet, splutter which made Katherine uncomfortable. Was it unwise to sit so near, when he was still so unwell?

Arthur inhaled a ragged breath, wheezing to verbalise his dream aloud, "You looked beautiful," he said, "You looked happy."
Katherine's eyes stung to think she would likely soon return to Spain if Arthur did not pull through. And she realised with a gut-wrenching ache that, though she missed her former life, she did not ever want to return if it meant Arthur's demise.
She took his hand, frail as a bird's broken wing, and kissed his knuckles, "You will see me happy again. If only you make it through, we can be happy."
He breathed a serrated laugh then, "No," he said, with something like peace, "Destiny has claimed me. And I am ready to receive it."
Arthur whispered one final wish before darkness took him, a murmur so low and weak Katherine had to lean in closely to catch it. A sob escaped her but she nodded.
And then Arthur's body went slack, slipping back into a fitful sleep plagued with dreams he would never see come to pass.

Chapter 22

5th April 1502
Greenwich Palace, London

"Your Grace," the king's confessor whispered, gently shaking Henry by the shoulder.

With a start, Henry sat up, fear rising immediately in his chest like acid, which only burned fiercer at the sight of the man's distraught face.

"If we have received good things by the hand of God, why should we not receive evil?" the confessor said, causing the king's heart to constrict.

"What is the meaning of this?" Henry asked, looking around the rooms as though the walls could offer up a clue.

The older man licked his lips, his brows creasing with the heavy burden of conveying such a dreadful message.

"I bring news from Sir Richard Pole at Ludlow, Your Grace," he said, wringing his hands before him, "I am sorry to tell you that…Prince Arthur has died."

Henry's ears began to ring as though they had been boxed. He could no longer hear what the man before him was saying, though his lips continued to move at an alarming rate.

"Get the queen," Henry mumbled. Or at least he thought he did, "Get the queen!"

Lizzie entered but a moment later, her ladies hurrying behind her, carrying her robe. They placed it over her shoulders when she stopped at the door's threshold, frozen to the spot at the terrifying sight of her husband, rather than by the cold.

"What is it?" she asked, her eyes wide, her cheeks slack with angst, "What is it? Henry?!"

It was then that the king broke down, at the sound of his wife's voice calling his name, asking for an explanation.

He could not give her one, could not speak the words without them tearing out his insides.
And she knew it then. Without so much as a word spoken. She knew that her child – the one whose birth had promised so much – was gone.
And everything they had done to perfectly secure their dynasty had been for naught.

<u>Ludlow, Shropshire</u>

Arthur's body was cleaned and prepared for burial, but not before his final wish was carried out.
With the knowledge that he was dying, Arthur had whispered with the very last of his essence that he wished for his heart to be buried at Ludlow.
My home… he had sighed, before sinking back into the pillows. Katherine hadn't told anyone straight away, for at the time, there had still been a sliver of hope that he would wake up recovered.
But unlike Katherine, who had survived the Sweating Sickness by some miracle, Arthur was not so lucky, and on the evening of the 2nd of April, he had stopped breathing.
Katherine fell into a deep grief following the physician's declaration that the prince had passed, for not only had she been groomed to be Arthur Tudor's wife from babyhood, but she had also begun to truly care for the young man.
He had been a prince of great promise. A boy who had shown her and everyone around him nothing but kindness and compassion.
He had been a gentle soul. Someone who would have one day been an incredible king. After all, he had been born and sculpted for that exact role.
But now that dream that had been forged for over a decade would never come to pass.
For the weight of the crown was never Arthur's to bear.

End of Book 1

of the

Tudor Rose Legacy
Series

Author's Note

Thank you for reading His Name Was Arthur, the first book in my Tudor Rose Legacy Series about Henry VII and Elizabeth of York's surviving children.
Though this book is fiction, His Name Was Arthur is as historically accurate as possible, only having taken creative liberties for the purpose of dialogue, character's thoughts, and feelings.

I hope you enjoyed learning about Arthur's secluded and oftentimes lonely life, and that despite his early death – or more accurately, *because* of it – the Tudor dynasty evolved into the extraordinary period in history we are still so fascinated by 500 years later.

If you enjoyed this book, please make sure to read my other works. Or leave a review on Amazon/Goodreads so that other historical fiction lovers might enjoy it, too.